ST. BART'S WAY

ST. BART'S WAY

A STORY COLLECTION

Patricia Schultheis

Washington Writers' Publishing House
Washington, DC

THIS IS A WORK OF FICTION

COVER DESIGN and PHOTOGRAPH by Erick Kogler

BOOK DESIGN and TYPESETTING by Barbara Shaw

LIBRARY OF CONGRESS CATALOGUING-IN-PUBLICATION DATA
Schultheis, Patricia.
  [Short stories. Selections]
  St. Bart's Way : a story collection / Patricia Schultheis.
    pages cm
    ISBN 978-1-941551-09-7 (softcover : acid-free paper)
  I. Title.
  PS3619.C4768A6 2015
  813'.6—dc23

                                2015018716

Printed in the United States of America

WASHINGTON WRITERS' PUBLISHING HOUSE
P. O. Box 15271
Washington, DC 20003

St. Bart's Way is dedicated
to the memory of my parents,
Ralph and Clara Podufaly,
and to that of my husband, Bill Schultheis.

CONTENTS

The Haint   9

After the Service   25

The Crunch   42

The Assembly   50

Bellini's Brush   67

Firewalker   76

Prime Meridian   91

Abiding Blue Velvet   107

Bang!   123

Other Men's Sons   128

Near Sunset   145

Standards   155

The Other Betty   178

Final Note   196
Acknowledgements   197

In the deserts of the heart
Let the healing fountains start
In the prison of his days
Teach the free man how to praise.

In Memory of W.B.Yeats
by W.H. Auden

THE HAINT*

---◆---

HENRI

Mr. Stanley Payton always calls me Henry, and I have never told him otherwise. My mouth would not my folly be—a black child sucks that with his mother's milk.

To the women testifying with their upraised palms, the young men with their streetcar strut, the children chasing chickens, I am *Mr.* Henry, the honorific sitting on my shoulders like an old shawl. As much as my "Henry" has deceived Mr. Stanley, it has deceived them.

Perhaps that's my greater sin, deceiving my own people. I always thought certainty in old age would be my recompense for so much misery, but this morning, when I put my hand in my wisdom pocket, I felt only a hole.

I looked out the window and saw Mars stalking the sliver moon, and, now, this evening the leaves hang as still as ice. If I touch one, it will feel as dead as leather.

The artifice of my "Henry" must stop—dissembling is the tool of those who need it to survive. The testifiers, chasers, and strutters, they are the ones who must bob and grin letting all the Mr. Stanleys call them whatever they please.

But for me, "Henry" is a burden. I want to lay it down. I want to own what's mine. I want Henri, the name my mother

---

*A term from Gullah, the language spoken on the barrier islands of South Carolina, and meaning a ghost, spirit or specter.

gave me, the name she called me in the secret of this little house in the back end of the Payton property.

Once a house slave on Lake Pontchartrain, but later a free woman, she carried her headful of French north to Baltimore along with her Bible, four silver spoons, and a blue velvet bonnet. On Baltimore's streets she walked with a prideful step and trailed a silk scarf of envious eyes behind her. But none dared criticize her because she worked for Mr. Harrison Payton whose son Stanley would have need of the ancient and indispensable art she practiced in the back room of our little house, a house that Mr. Harrison said would be hers forever.

She spoke French to me in secret—the testifiers, chasers and strutters, they would have rolled their eyes, not even bothering to hide their smirks. And white people, well, my mother was suspect enough.

The French, like the reading and beautiful script I learned from her, girded her secret dream for me. At night, alone, we'd work, my mother pinching my arm, saying, "Henri, *fais attention! Tu écoutes? Fais attention!* A man can carry a fortune in his head. He can use it to make something of himself."

But, for all her saunter, my mother could never give shape to her ambition. That "something" that I, a black boy in Jim Crow Baltimore, was supposed to make of myself remained as formless as the clouds. And over the years, my mother's insistence grew as weak as an invalid's tea. As if, on her trek from Louisiana, she had burned up a generation's worth of energy. And when she passed away, keeping the Bible for myself, I buried her with her blue velvet bonnet and four silver spoons and made myself as helpful to Mr. Harrison Payton as I could and then to his son, Mr. Stanley Payton, about whom I knew a thing or two.

I just stayed in this little house, finding, as the years passed, more wonder in the syncopated pods of woolly bears than in the source of the sun. Or in the beckoning stars.

I don't need much: my Bible, my little garden, my books, which I still keep hidden ... this little house. My days are rich, crammed with birdsong, the gray squirrels' flicking tails and randy ways. The turning of the willow by the stream where my mother bent to the ground and buried what she had to.

Before the testifiers, chasers and strutters hear them, the seasons speak to me. Soon after the winter solstice, beneath her snows, the earth pushes and I hear her groans. The solstice again, and the earth laughs, a full-throated woman having replaced spring's blushing girl. I hear the earth stirring her thunder. Snapping her lightning.

And now? ... this moment, what do I hear? A silence so solid a man can touch it. Not even the testifiers, for all the warm blood in their upturned palms, know what I do.

A mighty change walks this way. Yes, a mighty change.

It carries a silver-headed walking stick, perhaps the one it used upon the son who walks beside him. A father and his son. Mr. Stanley Payton the first and Mr. Stanley Payton the second, coming down to my little house. The two of them carrying change between them with such import it might as well be a cask of gold.

Mr. Stanley the first is florid-faced, gray-haired and black-browed. A roué, my mother would say. It is easy to see why the ladies loved him so. Still do, as I hear.

The son is a shadow, more so since he returned from the war. Small enough to begin with, he must have sliced off a piece of his self and buried it in a trench near the Argonne Forest. Whatever his father will have him do, his heart is not in it. Still, he is beside him, because that is what a Payton son does. As for Henri, I must forget him. I see this is not the time to claim what's mine, even if it is my true name. I slap a smile on my face and scarcely have time to tilt my head so my grin trickles down and dribbles off my chin. I step outside: *"Why Mista Stanley senior and Mista Stanley, young sir, wha you be doin' down heya? On this beautiful evenin', wha you be doin' comin' all the way down heya, 'cept to make an ole man happy?"*

GWENNIE

Exactly what am I doing that's supposed to be so wrong? That's what I want to know. It's not like I've got some God-awful disease and will infect everything.

When I open a client's closet, touch their clothes, what harm have I done? Not a single, solitary iota. So I count their loose change, the pills in their bathrooms, and I feel around to find how much cereal they've left in the bottom of the box. Not a thing is hurt. Not one single, solitary thing.

The truth is, as much as I hate to confess it, I love the risk. When I go through a client's laundry or touch their pajamas, I must feel something like that zone athletes say they feel. Or a doctor when he probes a comatose patient and knows more about that patient than the patient will ever know about himself.

Besides, I truly believe knowing about a client's private things makes me a better realtor—I know all their little secrets. For months, I've been prepared for the day Mr. Stram calls me into his office. I always imagine it's the younger Mr. Stram—Richie. He'll be pulling on his stiff cuffs—in the office Richie Stram never wears his suit coat, and his pants fit tight. He'll raise his fist to his mouth as if he were going to blow through it and clear his throat and he'll study the picture of his earnest little wife and daughters. Then he'll raise his eyes for a full blast of Gwennie and say that a client has complained. Things have been disturbed.

Then I will cross my legs and lay a little Carolina on him: "You know, Mr. Stram, I was afraid something like this was going to happen. There was this couple ... somehow I just didn't trust them further than you can toss a pig's ear. You're experienced; you know how you get a feeling for who's really serious, and this couple just didn't seem that interested. Then I heard someone else come in and I wanted to be sure to have them sign the book, so I left the first couple in the master bedroom. Why? Was anything missing?"

And, of course, poor little Richie Stram, suffering as he does under the yoke of his father, will just want the whole thing to go away. But I'll play the fiddle with my legs—I always invest in good stockings, the kind that swish when you cross them—and Richie Stram will clear his throat and say there must have been a mistake ... he doesn't want to keep me any longer.

No it's not a violation of the client's trust that worries me. It's the things that I touch ... am I violating *them*? ... leaving parts of myself on them? When I leave my fingertip cells on the scarves stacked in the corner of a widow's dresser drawer? My hairs on a divorcee's brush, the wet from my tongue on her teenage son's T-shirt, what have I left behind? Have the things I touched assumed some part of myself saying, "Gwennie was here. Gwennie was here."?

When I opened the house this afternoon, the rain was whipping so, I could hardly get the blue and yellow balloons tied to the For Sale sign—no one will come today. It's a pity. This house was once so elegant. Could be again. Solid plaster walls. Marble surrounds around all the fireplaces, the one in the living room with an overmantel. Italian tiles on the floors of both sunrooms. Double doors into the library. The windows have real mullions—all the houses around St. Bart's Way do. Not those cheesy snap-out ones McMansions have.

Still, I think, for all their good taste and money, the Paytons had secrets to drown. This was their house, and there's a sense of hard drinking here. An old shaker near the dining room wet bar and all kinds of glasses in the highboy. Cigarette burns on the carpet near the leather wingback and more on the wicker in the living room sun porch. And I noticed bottle rings on that linoleum-covered old shelf in the mudroom. If I put my tongue to them, I know I'd taste rum and bourbon. Maybe Maryland rye.

There's a haint in this house, I swear it. You can almost smell it.

The man who died here, Lawrence Payton, was the grandson of the original builder. This will be the first time the house will pass out of the Payton family—a selling point. People are so scattered these days, instant history seduces them. They think they can anchor themselves by living in the house of someone else's past.

Lawrence Payton must have lived here alone for some time after his wife died—that he was married I have no doubt—someone had to set the crystal candy dish near the green-silk sofa. And someone did the needlepoint.

But the contents of the medicine cabinet off the master bedroom have that scatter-shot approach I've noticed in other single men's. Almost everything, over-the-counter: nasal decongestants, daytime cold relief, nighttime cold relief, tubes of anti-inflammatories, four brands of aspirin, old ace bandages, an anti-itch ointment—no one to nag the poor man to get to a doctor.

Behind a box of digestion tablets I find three prescriptions.

All for Constance Payton. Restoril. Valium. And one for the medicine my mother took to keep food down during her chemotherapy. When I close it, the medicine cabinet makes a click. The house is so quiet, I almost wish the haint would talk just so I could hear something.

The rain is fierce, and even at two-thirty in the afternoon I need to turn on the bedroom light. I open Constance's dresser. All the things that touched her, her slips and bras and underwear, the things that would have retained her smell and molded themselves to the shape of her breasts and behind, are gone. I run my fingertips over the pale purple lining her empty drawers and smell. Lavender. Maybe its scent drove Lawrence mad with desire. Or maybe he never cared for it. Maybe he was the spice-and-jasmine sort but never told his wife. Maybe he told someone else.

I open his middle drawer and the labels on his polo shirts have the crossed-racquet logo of an old Baltimore shop. Neither Richard Stram senior or junior would buy shirts there, but the bankers financing the mortgages for the houses they sell do.

His T-shirts, I notice, are folded neatly, but are dingy. Maybe he washed them himself. Maybe he thought it would violate his modesty for a cleaning woman to handle them. What if she saw his chest hairs?

Something in back of the T-shirts rattles. I reach; it rattles again. My fingers touch a vial. Viagra! Did Lawrence use it to pleasure Constance? Or for someone after her? As if it makes a difference now.

Out the window the rain is battering the balloons—I'm certain no one will come. I take a T-shirt, press it to my cheek. It smells like old soap and something else, something raw. In the armpit. I close my eyes and lick it. I feel it getting wet from my tongue and know that my lipstick must be getting on it, but I cannot stop. I open my blouse and undo my bra and rub Lawrence Payton's wet shirt on my breasts. I put it between them and press them tight.

When I open my eyes the shirt is smeared with red, and I have no choice but to put it in my briefcase under Stram and Stram brochures. I swear this is the first time I've ever taken anything. I just touch things. I just touch.

HENRI

The Messrs. Stanley Payton stand with their legs apart and firm not three yards from my front door. The older one smiles. I peer into his eyes and see uncertainty there: he knows that I have not forgotten his deepest secrets, sees that I remember the three women he brought to my mother in the night.

But he does not know if this knowledge has given me power; that is his uncertainty. The air is so still I can almost hear his thumb as he rubs, rubs, rubs the silver head of his walking stick.

"Hello, Henry. Nice evening, isn't it? ... beautiful evening."

"*Yessir. Yessir. That it is. Very fine evenin'.*"

"You getting on all right these days, Henry? I just wanted to make certain."

"*Yes sir, Mr. Stanley. Ole man like me don' need much. I gets on just fine.*" The younger Stanley Payton clears his throat. I breathe deep and inhale the scent of rye—now I know his secrets as surely as I know his father's.

"You've ever been on the streetcar, Henry? ... The one where the line ends near the Presbyterian church?" the older Mr. Stanley says.

"*Oh once or twice, Mr. Stanley. The Presbyterian church, that's*

*quite a ways for an ole man. An' I don' have no need to go ridin'
around. Nothin' I need."*

"Well, that's what I've come to tell you, Henry. They're
going to be extending the streetcar line out this way. I wanted
you to hear it from me before the surveyors come. The line is
going to come right about where we're standing now."

*"You don't say, Mr. Stanley. Right about where you're standin'
now, you say?"* Whatever smile I had has dribbled away and
I'm careful to replace it with wide-eyed disbelief. My mind is
scrambling to use what I know about the older Stanley Payton
so I can stop the change I sense tunneling my way.

*"But why do they want to bring the line out here? Aint nothin'
out here. Me? Well, I don't need no streetcar."*

The younger Mr. Stanley shifts his weight a little and clears
his throat again. He has the studied movements of a man playing sober—I've seen it in the strutters. The older one says, "It's
not just streetcars that are coming, Henry. We're going to build
houses out here. Fine, fine houses. We already have the plans.
All over these hillsides and down to the stream—what you'll
see are beautiful houses. We even have a name for the principal
street ... someplace in the Caribbean where Mrs. Payton's
brother keeps his boat." He turns to his son: "What's it called?"

"St Bart's."

I look in the younger Mr. Stanley's eyes, but they are dead
to this. If I were to snap a twig he'd bolt like a deer. Three years
and still war-spooked.

*"All this is comin' heya? Fine houses and the streetcar, too?
Right by my little house?"*

"That's why we've come to see you, Henry. We need to see
your deed. We need to know exactly where your property line
is. We need to see your deed."

*"Oh, Mr. Stanley, you know I don' have no deed. Your father,
Mr. Harrison, he gave this little house to my mother, an' I just stayed.*

*So long as the Lord gave me strength I worked for Mr. Harrison an'
then for you. You know that, Mr. Stanley."*

"I know that, Henry, and you were a good worker, too. But
that was a while ago. Times change. We just need the deed to
check the property line, that's all. Just the property line. Isn't
that right?" He turns to his son.

"That's right. We just need to check. That's all," the son
says. He clears his throat.

And then I know what I must do. The leavings my mother
scooped, she buried by the stream. Oh, I know what I must do.
Only a sliver moon last night; only a sliver moon tonight. No
difference. I am an old man so blind I can see in the dark. I am
eager for them to go. I want to get to the stream, to Mother Willow, to what I know is buried beneath her. To touch it.

GWENNIE

I honestly don't care that many of the women buying houses
around St. Bart's Way are younger than I am. Most of them
were born old — tight-lipped and dull-haired — doctors,
lawyers, who can't buy a handbag worth of style for all the
money they earn.

When they're poking in closets or mentally measuring
windows for swags, I see their husbands glance my way and I
try to give the poor men something for their thirty years worth
of mortgage payments. I give them a full Gwennie when I bend
over to show how the fireplace damper works or reach to show
how the windows were rehung.

It fascinates the husbands that I know such things. As if a
realtor couldn't have some college. As if she couldn't have a
surgeon for a father who's owned houses this fine, or finer.

In fact, during the brief time he was married to the woman

I called Mommy Moron, my father's house was on the Charleston Showhouse Candlelight tour. My friends would come over just to snicker while Mommy Moron, skinny as a spider, harangued the painters and paperhangers. We were supposed to be doing our trigonometry or French, but we'd be watching her lay out upholstery samples in this light and that.

"Girls," she'd say, "which do you think? Now, remember, it's for a candlelight tour. It must look good in *candlelight.*"

And just to watch her spaz, Krista would pick the *fleur de lis* damask, and Allison the cut velvet. That fall, we drove Mommy Moron to tuck up her legs into her favorite yellow linen armchair and her second martini before Daddy pulled in the driveway.

Allison, Krista, and I were all drinking the afternoon Mommy Moron's son came home from the Citadel. Even with his tunic unbuttoned, Donovan looked sharp. Dark haired and broad chested. We were laughing—I don't know about what —maybe about the Showhouse Tour, when I spilt my drink, bourbon all over the champagne-colored couch.

I didn't know what to do; but Donovan just sat there. "It's okay, Gwennie. It's okay. I'll just tell Mom I did it … I made Dean's List and I'm Battalion Commander: she'll let me get away with anything. Even that stain."

"You'd do that for me?"

He smiled. "You're my stepsister, aren't you?"

When Allison and Krista left, he was still smiling. "Come here, Gwennie."

"Maybe we can just turn the pillows over."

"Come here, Gwennie." I heard him pull his zipper down. "Do you know all organs are organs of touch," he said. "You'd touch my ear, wouldn't you? My arm? Why not touch this? Just come here and touch it. It's just another organ. That's all you have to do. Just touch it. I won't touch you unless you want me to. Come here, Gwennie."

I don't know why I should think of that now. Maybe it's the rain. Or the haint I feel blowing through my hair like air stirred by leather wings.

If I cough, or make the bedsprings creak, the silence will shatter like a crystal vase.

I should see if the attic leaks. The roof is slate; beautiful, but hard to repair. I need to know if there are any holes ... what's coming through.

HENRI

I learned a thing or two of my mother's silver-spoon ways. When Mr. Stanley's scatter-brained wife was showing me how to set the chairs for her spring cocktail party, the hired girl stepped away from the silver she'd been polishing. A repoussé serving spoon caught my eye. Big and inelegant. Quick as a hawk to a rabbit, I took it.

All these years, I never knew why. Until tonight, when I take it to the willow by the stream.

It has not rained for weeks and the earth is hard. To soften it, I scoop water from the stream—willow leaves to stream's water; stream's water to willow's roots. I scoop.

When the spoon begins to bend, I claw my way—repoussé, useless as well as ugly.

I don't know what I am even looking for ... all those bones ... all those baby bones my mother scooped from those three woman Mr. Stanley brought to our little house, they would be gone by now, sucked into the marrow of their Mother Willow. Sprung into the glory of leaves, washed away by Father Stream.

But, still, I dig, my fingers, searching the soil for something that testifies to a life ended before it began.

I touch something. A rag…rags. That would be the last one he brought. A young thing, blonde, frail-boned. The sort of girl working behind a counter for her father or uncle and waiting for her destiny to cross a threshold and ring the little bell over the door. When Mr. Stanley handed her over, wide-eyed with terror, to my mother, she might have been a loaf of bread, a bag of biscuits.

With that last one, worse than the moans and screams was the silence. And then blood. So much blood, all her sisters before her might have pumped theirs into her and she was losing that too.

"Sheets, sheets," my mother said, and I was ripping as fast as I could, then going into the little back bedroom for more, tearing them off the bed, seeing the flash of Mr. Stanley's silver flask in the moonlight. Moonlight, too, later, when we buried the sheets.

They are old and rotted now and might tear if I rip them from where my mother buried them, so I clear the earth away carefully with the Paytons' spoon. I cannot tell if the stains on them are blood or dirt

When they are free, I will have to braid them so they hold. The Paytons want my deed—I will give them my deed.

I will wrap braided sheets stained with Payton blood around an arm of Mother Willow. And leap. My feet to Father Stream. My neck to Mother Willow. Let my last thought be a curse lasting beyond any memory of its cause. The curse the Bible gives—the one to the fourth generation. Let the Paytons have that for their deed.

GWENNIE

Once my mother was married to a man she told me to call Daddy Austin. On rainy Saturdays, especially if Mama had a luncheon or something, Daddy Austin would let me play in the attic. Sometimes I pretended a ghost was chasing me and I just ran from one end to the other, but Daddy Austin never said a word about the racket. Only Mama did, when she came home, calling from the bottom of the stairs, "Gwennie, you are going to wake the dead. Come down here, now. I brought the table favors, come see." And Daddy Austin would be smiling behind her as if he, too, had done something a little naughty. I was sorry to see him go. He was the only one to send me a note when Mama passed away. Sorry for my loss, he wrote, and that he was living in Houston.

I wonder if Lawrence Payton ever played up here. There certainly is room. The whole expanse is floored and gabled—it could have been bedrooms, except there are so many below, there's no need—even the maid's room is below.

The rain on the slate is the rain's own sound, the cry of drops. The slate is silent. Maybe it knows it can't win. In water over stone, water will always win. It just takes time. I listen for another sound, the steady plop of water on wood … the sound of a leak. But there's none. For, now, at least, the roof is tight.

Everything has been cleared out, probably to an auctioneer's, except for a cardboard carton far under one gable. Even in this dreary light, I can see its sides have begun to sag. Its corners, edges, haven't been crisp for years.

The only thing in it is an old brown accordion folder tied with a frayed gray cord. I work at the knot until it gives—my nails are naturally strong, and I have my manicurist double coat—my polish never chips. The pile of newspaper clippings I pull out might as well be dried leaves, they're that frail.

All of them are about a single life. Stanley Payton the Second's. The first article has a picture; he's wearing a blazer and white slacks and is standing with his Princeton classmates. He's smiling but not as broadly as the others. The next says that on the night before he went off to the First World War, his parents gave a party. A hundred and fifty guests, oysters, crab, fresh strawberries and Baltimore Lady cake. There was a band with a Negro singer.

When he was wounded and came home, he recuperated with his uncle down on St. Bart's. They watched a regatta.

And, then, there's his wedding. A small girl, tentative, like himself. I wonder what pressure, if any, did she feel when Stanley Payton the Second spooned his body around hers to cut the cake. Next, the announcement of their baby son, Lawrence. Then, one that Stanley has been elected secretary of the Baltimore Chamber of Commerce. Another, to the board of a hospital. The board of the symphony. All those years, the same haunted eyes.

I can't tell how old he is in the last. Maybe forty? ... fifty? It's a studio shot, appropriately dignified for the story: **Heir to Real Estate Fortune Ends Life**. "Yesterday afternoon, Stanley Payton, World War I hero, and heir to a real estate firm founded by his father, ended his life in the family home on St. Bart's Way ... ."

The clipping is weightless. I can't feel my fingers letting go when I put it in the folder. Or when I tie the cord. I don't feel even the knob when I pull the attic door shut. Or the railing under my palm as I go down the stairs.

The whole house—those rings on the linoleum-covered shelf, those cigarette burns—testifies to the secret of that dusty folder. Why did Lawrence stay here, in this home, for so long? Did he think he could outlive memory?

The rain is beating harder, and I don't hear the front door

open—only voices. A mother, father and two little boys are standing in the foyer, all of them dripping, and slightly breathless, as if surprised to find themselves there.

The father smiles: "Whew, I'm glad you're still here. The ad said 1 to 3. We're cutting it close, I know … a colleague of mine in Cleveland said 'If you're moving to Baltimore, you should check out the houses around St. Bart's Way,' but we almost didn't make it … we got caught in traffic … the Ravens game. And Timmy, here, came down with a stomach ache."

Without fresh lipstick, I feel half myself, but I give him my best smile.

"You all take your time. There's no rush. I'm in no hurry."

The mother is fussing with the little boys' dripping hoods, so I have no choice but to extend my hand to the father.

"I'm Gwennie Aldridge. And I just think it's a pity that you all came to Baltimore on the one God-awful day we have a year." The man, ruddy-faced and lanky, laughs. His hand is large and cold. And when he lets mine go, his nails trail down my palm to my fingertips; his thumb, the last to leave, slides over the red smooth nail of my middle finger.

From the foyer, the mother is looking into the living room. "Remember, boys, I told you not to touch anything." Her tone is full of admonition, but from her eyes, I can tell that she's already set Christmas candles on the sills and holly on the mantle.

Out the window, I see a yellow balloon has broken free. Like a big old implacable moon, it rises against the rain.

AFTER THE SERVICE

F unny. As a kid I never noticed the azaleas running riot across the back yards of St. Bart's Way. But after the service for Uncle Pete, my father's younger brother, I stare at the flowers outside the kitchen windows—anything to avoid my mother's eyes jitterbugging around the kitchen.

"Where is he?" She looks first to me, then my wife, then my sister Gail. In the center hall, the guests are arriving: the librarian who lived downstairs from Uncle Pete; my mother's sister and her husband; neighbors and friends. My mother wants to welcome them—her hostess turn always has been flawless and she needs my father to serve drinks at the makeshift bar. But as soon as he had turned into the driveway, my father and his old newspaper buddy headed to the garage with Pete's veteran friends.

"Where is he?"

"They went to the garage," says Gail.

"The garage? What's he doing there?" My mother's eyes oscillate with exhaustion—when I had come down for coffee at dawn I found her cutting roses in radishes. I had wanted to take her blood pressure, but she laughed me away. Doctor or not, I was still her little boy.

"Maybe he just needs to recoup. Who knows?" Gail says.

"Put a butter knife with the mustard and use that small Lenox bowl."

"I'll see what I can do," I say, grabbing a bag of chips and looking at my wife. A Midwesterner, Kara has never witnessed Baltimore's riotous spring. The flowers masking the stone foundations have renewed some essential calm robbed by my uncle's funeral. Once again I offer a prayer for having found this long-legged woman from the land of practical people. In the back yard, our young sons have wilted into the weathered chaise. The constraint of the funeral has blanched the color from their faces.

I reach for the knob of the side garage door: Drew, our oldest, sliding his six-year-old hand under mine; Frank, three, following.

Even as a child, the door to our garage was the door to mystery: cartons of motor parts, paints, shovels—my father always complained that he never could find a shovel with the right heft—mowers, rakes, fertilizers, and, of course, newspapers. Back then, I would run my fingers over them, hoping their secrets would transform my hands into those of a man. The light from the window silhouettes a circle of men. My father stands near the workbench along the back wall. Above it hang tools—the screwdrivers graduated according to size—hammers, saws, pliers, clippers, an ax; each hung with some good intention.

Charley Anson, my father's buddy, and three men from Uncle Pete's Vietnam veterans group are with my father who has found an intricate fishing reel, its tissue only a step from dust. A compact man whose eyes are the blue of the Irish Sea, my father seems desperate to put his hands on something finely honed, something well-balanced and running smoothly.

"You know, they're cleaning up the Inner Harbor," he says. "They say we'll be catching rockfish down there soon." Forty years in Baltimore and his voice still has the burr of Boston. "Thought I might go down there mornings. On the other hand,

I may just drop some chicken necks in a crab pot and see what I get. What do you think?"

"I caught a perch the other morning off Thames Street," answers a vet in a bolo tie.

My father rummages through some cartons. He pulls out a Volkswagen horn, a can of flea spray, a broken faucet, a basketball pump, and, finally, a bottle of Maryland rye. The liquor lights to amber as he holds it to the appreciative eyes of the waiting men.

"Darn," he says, "I knew I'd like fishing."

"Seems like you've got a knack for it," says Charlie Anson.

My father takes a white handkerchief and wipes a plastic lid from an aerosol can, taking special care with the tiny plastic ridges at the rim. Then does the same with others so everyone can drink.

I wonder if the precision he invests in the simplest task has its roots in his training in Latin—the precise conjugation of ancient verbs. His schooling by the Jesuits has given him a courtliness that served him well in a town where Southern probity rules. Too, my father has a hypnotic way with a story: a respect for the enduring power of words—qualities that once won him entry into Baltimore's inner chambers, those usually closed to a boy from Boston College.

"I think I'll have a Coke," says Lenny, the vet in the bolo tie, his voice croaking with longing and resolve.

"Coke sounds fine with me, too," says Charlie Anson, a vet himself.

My father sends Drew into the house for Cokes and the men fold round the bottle, their eyes searching for an object so as to hide their anticipation.

"You've got some fine poles," says Lenny, noticing old rods across the rafters.

"You want a fishing pole?" Charlie Anson asks Frank.

"I need one for Drew. He's my brother," Frank chirps. My father's eyes contract at the stab of "brother." He starts as if he feels some hand reaching on a dark tenement stairway.

Raised alone by my grandmother Nora, my father and Pete had only each other. For of all the mysteries, commandments, sacraments, and deadly sins Nora knew, she learned best the six-word admonition, "Spare the rod, spoil the child." That faith she practiced to perfection.

Drew runs across the lawn with the Cokes and my father pours them to the men nursing their sobriety and pours the rye for the others with a ceremonial flair. He hands the drinks to the circle of men and boys, and, with his plastic cup, salutes. The circle returns the gesture.

"To men who jump to the sky," says my father.

"To paratroopers."

"To Pete."

"To Pete."

"To Pete."

My parents rarely mentioned Pete after I was ten, but before that my uncle was very much the subject of conversation. "Should I ask your brother?" my mother would ask whenever a holiday or birthday neared.

She came from a large family whose manner of regarding each other as friends as well as relatives was profoundly genuine. At those innumerable gatherings, those birthdays, holidays, baptisms, some current affirmed their essential decency.

My mother considered the meagerness of my father's family a pity and saw her attempts to encircle his brother in hers as something that could only be enriching, for my uncle's life careened between a veteran's hospital and a second floor apartment on Lanvale Street.

If Pete were on Lanvale Street, my parents—and I can still remember them sitting at the kitchen table—would discuss who was coming, and who was not, since my uncle could not tolerate surprises. Not even loud noises.

Whatever the occasion, he always came early and ensconced himself in the blue wingback chair to the right of the fireplace. I believe those times, while my mother fussed and padded about in her slippers before putting on her dress shoes, were the richest domestic scenes Pete ever witnessed.

When the others came, Pete was unfailingly polite, even engaging, always remembering everyone's name, where they worked. He shared my father's intelligence and knack for surprising metaphors. He too had a gift for the long tale and an Irishman's wry, self-deprecating humor.

And my mother's family, treasuring civility as they did, chose to overlook the restless way Pete's eyes moved, his reflexive habit of smoothing his hair and clearing his throat. They were good-hearted people, who had honed graciousness to an art, so they regarded putting Pete at ease as evidence of their own virtue.

Pete, however, would never leave the blue wingback chair. Not even to shake a hand. Only an abrupt rending of the social hubbub—the sudden shattering of a glass, a too-loud laugh— could propel him from that blue cocoon. Then he would rise suddenly, his eyes scanning the crowd for his brother.

I remember the New Year's Day my father was talking with my Uncle Warren about trickle-down economics; they were at the dining room table where a ham sat like a doomed potentate. Never missing a beat, my father turned toward his brother who was just rising from the blue chair: "Ready to go, Pete?"

"Ready as I'll ever be."

And the sound of the party almost drowned out the Volkswagen backing down the drive.

In the garage my father refills the glasses of the solemn circle, but I cover my plastic cap with my palm and step into the yard. The noontime sun has ratcheted up the gaudiness of the flowers, and I understand why Pete once called them "Jell-O-mold flowers"—middle class and proud of it.

I go into the kitchen where my mother's older sister, my Aunt Louise, is filling tiny sandwiches with shrimp salad. She makes three, slips a spatula beneath, and slides them—one, two, three—onto a silver tray, her smile spreading all the while. "These should lure those men in from that garage."

I suppress the temptation to mention the latest article on cholesterol in *Lancet*: "Your famous shrimp salad, Aunt Louise?"

"Well, it is the least I could do. What with you mother having a houseful and all. Besides, I was really very fond of your uncle."

"Is that a fact?"

"Why, yes. Of course." I calculate quickly; it is over fifteen years since Louise and Pete had been in my parents' home together.

"Where's Mom?"

"The last I saw, she was in the living room, talking to that librarian."

I wander into the dining room where Kara is talking about ceiling molding with my uncle Warren, Louise's husband. When she lifts her arm in a sudden balletic motion, my wife's thrall sifts over my uncle as surely as a net.

These genteel exchanges mingle with the harmonics of silver, china, and crystal and remind me of the cordiality some of my most seriously ill patients assume—the extra effort they make to ask about my sons or how I'm coping with winter in Minneapolis. Civility served in the face of sorrow always has struck me as somehow both fitting and brave.

My mother, her smile brittle with earnestness, pauses in telling Mary Gleason, the only black person in the room, how she "adores" Alice Walker. Her eye catches mine, but I ignore the question her glance holds; she wants to know if my father has come in from the garage.

I reintroduce myself to Mary and we chat about the difficulty of flying to Baltimore with two small children. She still has the slender elegance I recall from the times my father and I visited Pete on Lanvale Street. Her closely cropped hair has turned gray and enhances the symmetry of her head and her long neck. She is wearing dramatic, oversized glasses and a gray shawl draped over a simple black dress. The rye is with me and I want to be near Mary's center point of utter calm. All about her might be chaos, but in Mary there are only symmetry and balance. An arresting woman, this Mary Gleason.

"Well, the trip wasn't too bad. We flew. We've flown quite a bit because my wife's parents live in Duluth."

"Yours are thoroughly modern children, are they?"

"Very modern. Sometimes, I think too modern." And then, unable to hold it back any longer, "I just want you to know I have a book that you gave Pete a long time ago."

"Oh, Pete—he was a great reader. And very eclectic. I loved that about him. He wasn't stuffy at all. Some people look down on the newer writers; they think no one can live up to the great classics. But not Pete. He was open to anything."

"Oh I'm afraid this is one of those older ones. It's *Anna Karenina*."

"Ah, his favorite. One of his many favorites, I should say. One of mine too."

"I just wanted you to know, I've kept it over fifteen years."

"And you've actually read it?" she said smiling.

"Once. Once was enough," I laugh. "When I was fifteen."

That summer my father took me to the veterans' hospital. I think he wanted to show me that just when the horizon seems endless, time slips away from you, and you become an onlooker to the only life you'll ever have; at fifteen I was as rootless as the dandelion puffs my sons chase.

The hospital was on a spit of land stretching into the upper Chesapeake. Perhaps it was hoped the undulating shoreline grasses could coax peace into splintered souls. Men with stubbled chins and pastel robes lined the corridors. I remember thinking, "These are baby colors: pink, pale green. Why do these men wear these colors? They were soldiers. Why dress them like babies?" Their harrowed eyes studied the bay's shimmering surface as if it were a Ouija board.

At the end of the corridor Uncle Pete was alone in a room lit by windows reaching almost from floor to ceiling. He had fashioned a chaise by pulling up a chair to face the one he sat in and stretched out his long legs.

"Christ Almighty and all the saints, will ya look at what the cat's dragged in!"

"Don't get up. We only just drove sixty miles," my father said.

"I won't. Why? You don't want a chair, do you? After a drive like that, it'll do you good to stand for an hour or so. Strengthens the legs. That's why they don't have pews in the great cathedrals of Europe. Stand through a year of High Masses and you're ready for anything. All the best crusaders had legs like iron. It's a fact."

"You're full of it."

"That may be, but I'm not the one with tired legs, am I?" Pete stretched out further.

"What are you reading?"

"Something better than that tref you publish, unless you want to put Tolstoy up there with some wacko columnist."

"You still trying to read *Anna Karenina*? Christ, Pete, you've been tryin to read that since you were sixteen."

"Actually it's Kitty, Jack, she turns me on. Kitty and those high heels of hers. But listen to me talkin about bein' turned on in front of a wee tiny innocent such as we have here. How old are you now? Nine? Ten?"

"Fifteen." I knew he was kidding, but still, it felt raw.

"You wouldn't be lyin to me now?"

"No, Uncle Pete. Honest. I'm fifteen."

"Ah, that's okay. It's only a wee bit of a fib. Go to confession. Don't worry about it."

"Really. I'm fifteen."

"Then you must have the stunted growth curse that runs through our family. You've told him about the stunted-growth relatives in Ireland, haven't you, Jack?"

"Actually, I'm five-ten."

Pete grinned at me from his makeshift chaise. "Tell him, Jack. The poor souls with the stunted growth curse, most of them do just fine. People generally have more sense than to confuse them with leprechauns. And if they do, they'll pay for it because the leprechauns take great offense. You'll hit your growth any time now."

"Really, I'm five-ten, Uncle Pete. And that was three months ago. I might have grown even more since then."

"Yeah. Yeah. By whose yardstick? That apostate school you play basketball for? I read about it in that rag of a paper of your father's. St. Paul's is it? What can you expect? A school with English leanings if ever there was one. It's a fact they use them foreshortened yardsticks. Goes with their peckers. Still, I guess St. Paul's is okay for someone with your unfortunate genes. Don't you think?"

I shrugged.

"You better get him a specialist, Jack. He could be having

a seizure of some sort. Fine young man like this—doesn't look you in the eye. Twitches instead of sayin' 'Yes' or 'No.' It's a damn shame. Could be the stunted growth. A damn shame. A fine boy like this, just about to hit his growth."

I tell Mary how relieved I had been when my father finally set down a bag of books she had sent. And I remember how happy Pete was as he read each title: *Washington Square; I, Claudius; Emma*; and, last, another copy of *Anna Karenina*. Pete gave it to me and I accepted it, just so I wouldn't hear any more about stunted growth.

And I tell her how, when I saw Pete and my father out on the seawall, they reminded me of the halves of a seed, but I never tell her how, when we got home, the phone rang just as my mother asked about Pete. Before my father could reply, my mother answered it and spent the rest of the evening chatting with Aunt Louise.

Mary and I talk about other books Pete loved and just when I'm about to tell her I plan to reread *Anna Karenina*, Frank's howl of anger and pain pierces the white noise of sociability. Kara is down the steps and across the lawn before I am through the kitchen door.

"Drew threw a brick at me," Frank wails.

"I did not. You put your hand in the way, you little stupido."

"That's enough." Kara holds Frank close, but the three-year-old is too angry to let her see his hand.

"We would have had him if you hadn't put your hand in the way, you little stupido."

"That's enough I say." Kara tries to cuddle Frank's head to her shoulder. I examine his hand. The bones are so flexible, they're not so much bones at all as the promise of bones. But the skin is abraded. Kara carries him into the house, and I turn to Drew.

"He put his hand in the way. I told him."

"Told him what?"

"To move."

"What were you doing?"

"Looking for a snake."

"Where?"

"There." A pile of bricks along the garage has been pulled apart. "We wanted to get him and bring him home."

"How were you going to do that?"

"We were going to ask Grandma for a jar."

"Is everything okay over there?" my father calls from the driveway.

"Fine," I answer just as Uncle Warren steps onto the porch and lifts a silver tray with tiny sandwiches over his head like a winning athlete. He heads toward the brotherhood of the garage.

"Why don't you go get a sandwich?" And as Drew trots across the yard, I go to check on his brother. As I pass through the kitchen, my mother repeats her lament, "Isn't he ever going to come in? There are people here."

"He knows that, Mom. There are people out there too."

"Well, you know what I mean. It's just that he should come in."

"He's just tired, Mom."

"And will you look at that?"

"What?"

"Your Uncle Warren. He's just laid that tray right on the drive. Nothing under it. Your Uncle Warren just laid the silver tray smack on the driveway," she says to Gail — a sort of pop quiz that I've noticed mothers spring on daughters.

"The one from Grandma?" Gail asks on cue.

"For our anniversary," my mother finishes. I go upstairs to check Frank's hand.

Kara is sitting on the rim of the tub, rocking him; her eyes tell me all is well. Out the window, on the driveway, I hear the men, their conversation a current of repartee.

"This party could use some pickles," my uncle Warren says. "So happens I've got some in the car." A car trunk slams and then Warren asks, "Did I say 'pickles'? Damn, I meant 'pickled.' Amazing what a difference one letter can make. Age will do that to ya." I don't have to look out the window to know he's unearthed another bottle. Charley Anson says he could use another Coke and asks Lenny if he wants one too. My father sends Drew for paper cups.

The talk turns to the condition of the driveway that runs between my parents' yard and their neighbors' the Cottmans. Lenny tells my father that he's worked on a road crew, and laying a good driveway isn't as easy as it looks; there are all sorts of things to consider: drainage, roots, shade, sun, sewer lines. All sorts of things. My father starts asking him easy questions and then focuses on drainage when it's clear Lenny knows what he's talking about.

"You want to minimize any slant toward your basement. If it has to go anywhere, let it go towards your neighbors. Of course, you don't want no lawsuit neither. The important thing is the slant and how deep for a well-laid drive."

"If he's talkin' about deep and well-laid, ya know he's lyin'," says another vet. "He don't know nothin' about deep and well-laid."

"Better to lie about deep and well-laid than tell the truth about short and sorry like you, you miserable old peckerwood," Lenny says.

Kara looks out the bathroom window. "Why don't they come in? What are they all doing out there?"

Drew's voice drifts upwards: "Where are the pickles?" The men laugh and Frank stirs at the sound of his brother's voice.

"I'm all right, now."

"Maybe you should leave the snake alone for now," Kara suggests. But he's already gone to join his brother.

Kara and I go across the hall to the spare bedroom. The architectural details stand out: the well-proportioned dormer, the solid brass doorknobs, the eight-over-eight mullioned windows offering a unique perspective on St. Bart's Way. Kara runs her hand over the wide, common sill. "This millwork," she murmurs, "it's beautiful. So difficult to duplicate." Her fingers, like her legs, are long. Everything about my wife is straight and true.

I remember the Easter I had stood at that same window and watched my Uncle Pete walk away from the house on St. Bart's Way where he would never be welcome again.

"So what's going on? Why aren't they coming in?" Kara says. "Your mother, she must be having a fit. It's not like your father. What's going on?"

"I think it's because of Pete."

"What about Pete?"

"It's complicated."

"Yeah?"

"I think my father ... I think he may be protesting."

"Protesting what?"

"Against Vietnam." And so I tell her that I thought my father was not coming in as a protest against hospitality served to honor a brother who wasn't welcome.

I tell her about the surprisingly warm, rainy Easter when my father was late at the paper and my mother's preparations were especially elaborate—she had just inherited a set of fine china and she wanted to show it off.

Pete was in the blue chair; he had brought Gail a gray plush, lop-eared rabbit, and we were considering scurrilous names like Mr. Snotgot and Sir T. Tail Wigglesmore. Suddenly a noise loud enough to make the lilies on the dining room table trembled rolled through our house.

"What was that?" Pete's chest heaved.

"It's thunder, Uncle Pete." Gail's face puckered in bewilderment.

"That's not thunder," his voice hoarse.

"Yes, it is so." And then another clap.

"My god." He was out of the chair and clutching Gail to his chest. She started to cry; she had dropped the bunny. "My god, we've got to get out of here." Pete was trying to get my arm.

"It's just thunder, Uncle Pete."

My mother, in from the kitchen. "What's wrong? What is it?"

"We have to get out of here." Still holding Gail, steering me into my mother, pushing me to her, her face ashen. Another clap. Pete thrusting me to my mother, making her stumble against the table.

"Move! Move! For Christ's sake. We'll be hit!"

My mother still uncomprehending. Frozen.

"Move!"

Still frozen. And, then, my mother, stumbling, grabbing the table cloth, and china—her very good china—cascading to the floor, all crash and clatter and shards.

"No! No, Pete!"

And another clap. "Christ, they're close. We've got to get out." Pete's face red with rage at my mother's stupidity, trying to grab her.

"For God sakes, Pete. Put her down!" Gail screaming now. My mother trying to wrest her away. Me stumbling against her. Lightning so bright the silver caught it. Another clap.

And my uncle grabbing a knife. "Do as I say! We've got to get out. Christ, they're close. We've got to get out."

"My God, Pete! My God. Put her down! Stop! For the love of God! Stop! "

And suddenly rain sheeting against the window, my uncle pressing his palm against the pane, and then turning to my mother, grief contorting his body. And then sinking to the carpet. And burying his face in the corner of the linen tablecloth. And Pete sobbing.

And sobbing still as I took Gail by the hand up the stairs to the room with its unique perspective on Bart's Way. And maybe sobbing still as I watched him slowly walk away. And maybe still when my father's Volkswagen turned the corner, made a U-turn, and Pete got in. And all the while hearing those other sobs, the ones of my mother as she and Aunt Louise picked up shards of china. And my mother groaning, "He had a knife, Lou, a knife."

When I finish, Kara's eyes resolve that nothing like that will ever happen to her sons. I enfold her and think how frail we are when measured against the times we are born to. And when she pulls away, the flash of an ankle bracelet shows in the swirl of my wife's skirts.

By the time I come downstairs, the men have wound their way down the drive to the front of the house. My father and Lenny are talking about roofs, Lenny saying that replacing a roof does no good at all unless your gutters are good. He knows; his brother was a roofer and most roofing problems start with gutter and downspout problems. He has a slight man's agility and leaps onto the porch's broad railing. Holding on to the gutter, he inches his way along, commenting about water damage, rotting shingles and rust, and just when he is across from the front door, my mother, followed by Mary Gleason, opens it.

"Lenny, here, is giving me some roofing tips. His brother's

a roofer," says my father. I search his face for conciliation, but his eyes yield nothing. Such is his victory.

"Mary has to leave," my mother says, only her mouth smiling.

"Here, Mary, let me drive you," my father says, taking out his keys before my mother can object.

Charlie Anson is on a cell phone talking to the paper. He wants to use the corporate skybox for that night's ball game. "Yeah, yeah, a coupla vets here. Heroes, for Christ sake. Christ, you should see the decorations they have. I never seen such scrambled eggs. Golden bough clusters and everything." When he clinches the skybox, he turns to my father. "You comin, Jack?"

"Maybe we'll join you later. What do you say, Ned? We could take the boys." So the three of us get into the back of his car, Mary in front. My father is deferential, even tender towards her, holding the door and making certain her seatbelt is comfortable.

"The azaleas are especially vivid this year," she remarks, as he pulls away.

"Maybe the cool and rainy spring," he says. The streets gradually became wider, emptying their traffic onto a thoroughfare, a rib of commerce leading to a grand convergence at the harbor's edge. Only when the car has entered into a perfect syncopation of lights and speed do my father and Mary feel a dispensation to say "Pete."

"It was a lovely service."

"I think Pete would have liked it," says my father.

"I think so. Especially the piper."

"I had a devil of a time finding one. I can tell you."

"It was worth it."

"I was wondering, Mary, do you want the flag?"

"The flag? Oh, I don't know. I don't know what I'd do with it. Don't you want it, Jack?"

"I don't know. I don't know what I'd to do with it, either. It's in the trunk, for crying out loud. Heck of a place for it, but I just didn't know where to put it."

"Well, let me think about it. I wonder what people do with those flags. Put them on the mantle? In a drawer somewhere?"

"Might be an interesting story. I bet some people burn them."

"I bet they do. Oh, I bet they do."

When my father turns onto Lanvale Street, the house where Pete lived above and Mary lived below is dark. She turns to my father, "Well, I guess this is it. I guess it will be what it will be. Either a beginning. Or an end. But the truth is that I really only like endings in books. Other than that, I'm sort of a middle person."

"I know, Mary. So am I."

She waits as my father opens the car door for her and as he puts her key in her lock, ceding to him his need for chivalry, his need to act. And when he opens the door, the entry is as dark as the farthest reaches of memory.

Then my father drives down Lanvale Street, neither turning north, towards St. Bart's Way, nor south, towards the game. He can, I realize, see into the distance only as far as the next streetlight leads him. His hands on the wheel are brown-flecked with something surfacing. Something ineluctable and final. Something stronger than bone that one day will leave my father alive only in Gail and in me. And, then, only in my boys. At the corner, he slows and looks over his shoulder at them asleep in the rear. There, they rest. Boy limb over boy limb. Palms turned toward the gathering night. Brothers in repose.

THE CRUNCH

Having run to fat earlier in his thirties, Gordy had resigned himself to "portly." "Portly" was good. "Portly" imbued a lawyer with a certain trustworthiness. "Portly" swirled May morning air up the flap of the Saturday polo shirt hanging over Gordy's belly.

To a curbside musician's gravelly blues, the throng churned clockwise around the parking-lot farmers' market. Gordy sipped his coffee and watched Carla toss a few coins into the guitarist's tattered case. Whatever she said made the musician's rheumy eyes smile. She never looked at Gordy.

Gordy had noticed that about divorced women—their independence. Carla's, he had to admit, bordered on total indifference. But then, Carla had skipped the marriage and divorce business altogether, and proceeded directly to child support.

Gordy followed her process-tortured hair poking out of the back of a baseball cap. She took a bag of onions with the care she'd reach for an infant from a lowering lifeboat. She was the most focused woman Gordy had ever known. The way concentration condensed her little frame at baseball games. Her precision when she chopped vegetables. Even her sleeping was intense.

About the only thing Carla seemed casual about was himself. Sometimes Gordy thought she only saw him when they were going to bed; she would glance up from brushing that tangle of hair and look surprised, as if to say, "Oh, it's you! Well, hi there!" In the space of dresser to bed, Carla's eyes could shoot a million messages, not the least of which was something obdurate and absolute—"I don't trust you to stay." Even at baseball games she was wary, telling her little girl, "Abby, say 'Thank you' to Mr. Gordy for the cotton candy." And it was a standing joke between them that not Gordy, but Unitas, his woeful hound, bought the expensive steaks Gordy sometimes grilled in her sliver of a back yard.

Snow had brought them together. The office closing early, hushed in the backdraft of departure. But he, working on a big case, needed the best paralegal in the firm, only she couldn't stay; she had to get her little girl. And him saying out of the blue, "I can drive you. Take a laptop."—her oversized sweater and tights pushing the limits of office casual, her face a gnarl of worry. "I'll want at least time and a half. And don't expect much in the way of dinner. Chef Boyardee and me, we have a thing goin' on."

And so it went, over Christmas, bumping into Valentine's Day, and the awkwardness of not knowing what their gifts were supposed to signify until a mutual flu made that particular discomfort seem as graceful as a *pas de deux*. And discovering she really could cook, especially stew, if she wanted to, and that they both loved mysteries and the surprise of the daffodils she coaxed from that sliver of a yard of hers, and the heartbreak of Abby's ankles in lace-trimmed Easter socks. And then the opening day game they had tickets for, but found they had something much better to do. And here it was, nearly Memorial Day, and Gordy was no closer to knowing why he was with her than that evening he had taken his snowy shoes and socks off in her living room and smelled ravioli.

Still, after six months, you'd think she'd trust him enough

to at least let him help her with those bags. A summoning look would have done it. She was beside a long-boned woman in khaki shorts and a curtain of blond draping her face. When Gordy inserted himself between them, the woman lifted her hair. "Gordon? Gordy Hanson! Well, well. What is this? Old home week?" Meredith Cottman's hand was as soft as a pillow. "So Gordon, what brings you out this fine morning? Is it the apples or the oranges?"

A baseball cap nudged his arm. When he introduced her, Carla freed a hand from her bags in an eternity of awkwardness. She herself rescued them: "I'm going to get Abby some strawberries, Gordy. I'll meet you at the car," abandoning him to the wonder of blond that had distracted him so many years ago when he played prep school lacrosse with her brother Bruce. He and Meredith Cottman fell into those old familiar rhythms of well-bred wit and followed the clockwise churn: Who would have guessed it, old Bruce Cottman in bonds down in Houston? … helluva lacrosse player, old Brucie … and Meredith wasn't a "little" sister any more, was she? They both had mastered it many years ago, that high-style banter skirting flirtation. Little Meredith Cottman, her two vocabularies: English and French and neither of them having a word for "zit." They played catch-up: his career moves, hers; his family, hers. Their eyes tossing the hot-potato question: Why neither of them was married. Some disappointment had seasoned her, made her more beautiful. There was no denying it, after six months, there was something to be said for being the man beside the woman other men noticed.

When he reached her, Carla was leaning against his SUV with her phone. "We have to get Abby, my mother's new blood pressure medicine is acting up. She can't take Abby to T-ball."

The cup holder might have been a country club chaise for the comfortable way the essence of Meredith settled itself between them. "Come on, Carla. She was just somebody I knew."

But he knew that Carla knew the truth: that the people he knew and the people she knew, would never know each other. Even the streets testified to it: Inch by inch, the sidewalks, the row house yards, their valiant little shrubs, all shrunk.

"The game starts at eleven."

"I played lacrosse with her brother, for God's sake, Carla."

"I wasn't thinking of her, Gordy. I'm worried about my mother."

It was the natural time for a break. Her damned way of keeping him at arm's length. Never allowing him to sleep over unless her daughter was at the child's grandmother's, so what was he supposed to do? Spend Saturday nights alone watching videos with Unitas? She would know it for what it was: the six-month equinox, the time in a relationship cycle when the forces you've kept at bay hoping something would take root, converge. All the elements were aligned: Abby's coming home; the unexpectedness of Meredith. It was time: he would tell her after getting Abby at her mother's.

At the little kitchen table Gordy dissolved his second doughnut in black tar coffee and listened to Carla and her mother murmur in the living room. Could be Meredith they were talking about ... could be Shirley's new medication.

He had always taken Carla's mother, with her teddy bear sweat shirts, for a good-hearted soul, the sort of woman who ministers to the moment. Something like Carla, only with kindness. But now he wasn't sure. If he were a cynic, he would have considered Shirley's acid-roasted coffee a preemptive strike for his anticipated breakup with her daughter. Maybe Carla's mother had calculated, come up with her own relationship astronomy—mothers could do that.

Whatever, he was well out of it. All about him was evidence of what a life with Carla would be. The rooster and chicken salt and pepper shakers, a menagerie of refrigerator magnets, a clutter of coupons. Across from him Carla's little girl ate a bowl of cereal. "I got a loose tooth."

"What?"

"I got a loose tooth."

"You do?"

"Want to see?" And then she was before him, giving him no choice but to peer into her milk-slopped mouth, and watch her tongue wiggle the incisor back and forth in a susurrus squish while a trickle of blood stewed with flecks of cereal. What was she trying to do? Gross him out? Did they know to do that? At six? The child adjusted her glasses and looked at him expectantly.

"Does it hurt?"

"Only when I crunch my cereal."

"Well, the crunch can kill ya."

"Yeah, it can."

"Want the rest of my doughnut instead?"

Before she had taken three bites, she put it down: "Mr. Gordy?"

"What?"

"Thank you for the doughnut."

The tooth fairy was just on the tip of Gordy's tongue when Carla came in: they had to get going. It was getting late: the game started at eleven. Gordy countered with Unitas—he had been alone since last night, for God's sakes. Just imagine the mess he could make.

And he had. So there was cleaning that up and getting to the T-ball game just in time. And Abby actually making a catch —her first ever—and jumping up and down instead of throwing the ball. And Carla screaming from the bleachers, "Throw the damned ball, Abby!" And she did. So, of course he couldn't break up with her then, could he?

And not at McDonald's when Abby bit into her hamburger and her face puckered in consternation and pride: her tooth was out. And him watching Carla cup her hand under the little chin to catch the muck of burger and fries and plucking from it a dazzle of white that Gordy could only take as evidence of Mother Nature's profligacy. Why else replace what already was perfect?

And then they all were winding through the Saturday afternoon streets: Gordy, Carla, Abby, Unitas, and that other one, that long-boned homunculus lounging in the cup holder. He would do it, he told himself, as soon as they got to her house. He'd let Abby take Unitas for a walk—she was always asking to—and then he would do it.

It was more dangerous than he had expected—Carla started slicing the strawberries at the sink. Her index finger extended along the dull edge of the blade for better leverage. But what the heck, it wasn't like he hadn't done it dozens of times before.

"Carla, I've been thinking."

"Yeah."

"Well, I better be going."

"Yeah."

"I've been thinking, Carla."

"You said that, Gordy."

"Well we ... "

"Why don't you just come out with it, Gordy?"

"What?"

"Apples and oranges, right?"

He needed to regain the initiative but could only think of "What?"

"Us, Gordy ... you and me. Apples and oranges. Just like what's-her-name said. But we've always known that, haven't we? At least I did. It's not like I didn't know what you were going to say, Gordy." She kept slicing.

Gordy felt in his pocket for his keys. He wanted to say something significant. After all, it had been six months. And they certainly had had some good times. He couldn't deny it. And no one could say she had asked anything of him. She continued at the strawberries as if she had been preparing for this moment from the very beginning.

Funny, how small women sometimes were the bravest. A man could feel diminished by it. Gordy felt for his keys, but his fingers found instead the napkin holding Abby's tooth. Somehow he couldn't bring it into the open just yet. How astonishing that the tiny piece of perfection in his fingers had its origins, not in a little girl walking his dog, but in the woman before him at the sink. And in her mother before her.

He tried to imagine Meredith at a sink. There would have to be imported tiles, an Italian faucet, a restaurant-grade range and custom cabinetry—his partners would be coming for dinner—again. And all signifying some domestic perfection impossible to attain, at least by himself, but that wouldn't stop Meredith from a lifetime of making him try. All those holidays, those Christmases and christenings at her parents' on St. Bart's Way.

"Deal, Carla."

"What?"

"Deal?"

"You mean like a plea bargain?"

"If you want to call it that."

"What have you got in mind?"

"Your knife for Abby's tooth."

"I'd be nuts to take a deal like that, Gordy."

"Why?"

"You know for a lawyer, you've got lousy criminal in-stincts. A knife, I can throw, can't I? Then I'd have the tooth plus anything else I want. But what are you going to do with a tooth, Gordy? Send in the fairy? Get real."

Her eyes could shoot a million messages: it could take a man a lifetime to read them all. "Put the knife down, Carla," Gordy said. "And look at me." Even without the knife, her hands were blood red. But they smelled so sweet.

THE ASSEMBLY

Yellow is hard. And Mina knows colors. A good eye—the customers always said so. Twice she had her husband Marvin paint their old living room yellow. The first time, too gold; the second too lemony—she lived with it. But here, in these two rooms, well, they've gotten it perfect, her son and daughter-in-law. Even her old furniture seems relaxed. The mahogany sideboy under one dormer window. Her bookcase under another—all she needs. She's begun to crochet again. And she has her dog. Her radio. But no television. That she goes downstairs for. Sits with them—her son, his wife, her grandson.

And, of course, she's with them for meals—her daughter-in-law Rose takes such pains. It's getting better. Mina can't deny it. Not quite as awkward. She's learning. If she looks down into the garden and sees Rose picking the last of the mums, she goes downstairs, watches her filling a vase, talks about the colors. Says how good the flowers look on the mantle. It isn't much, but something: it's only been three months.

The only one who took to it naturally is her grandson. "Grandma's coming to live with us? Cool!" That's what her son Gary told her the boy had said.

Jason, God bless his dark brows, like those she and her sisters had, and, of course, their brother ... she's never told anyone that's what she sees in the boy. He stands, now, in the dormer window, luminous with youth-on-the-cusp. His eyes innocent that he's committed the worst sort of betrayal: that done with purity of heart.

"Will you do it, Grandma?"

"What?"

"Come to the assembly?"

"You told them I would?"

"I told them I'd ask."

"What did your teacher say?"

"Mr. Fitzhugh is in charge of Family Heritage Month. He's not really my teacher. He teaches physics. I'm not into physics."

Looking up at him, she knows he's little more than a bundle of adolescent urges, but, still, he retains enough sweetness to break Mina's heart. Her son and daughter-in-law have pinned such hopes on him—as if Mina, herself, weren't reminder enough that the future has less substance than smoke.

Every six weeks a report comes from the private school with a Latin motto and serpentine walks. A gloom settles over the house, floats up to Mina's yellow rooms. Gary will make that clicking noise with his tongue, and her daughter-in-law's face, cheerful at the dinner table, will collapse at the counter. The grades aren't bad, but not good enough for the college the boy's sister attends. The boy himself will shoot baskets off the garage until his father calls, saying the neighbors will complain.

"Well, what did this Mr. Fitzhugh say?"

"He said he understands."

Mina thinks no one named Fitzhugh could ever understand. "When does he have to know?"

"I forgot to ask."

She pushes herself up from her chair. All about are framed

photos of the life she lived as wife and mother: herself and Marvin on a cruise; the weddings of their daughters; Gary's medical school graduation: Marvin, on one side; Rose, not Mina, on the other.

"Do you think the boys will want to hear?"

"Well, yeah ... I mean it's like they have to be there any way. It's an assembly, you know."

"An assembly for the Holocaust?"

"Well ... yeah. They have one every year. It's Family Heritage Month."

"Every year, this Family Heritage Month includes something about the Holocaust?"

"Just about."

"And someone comes to talk?"

"Well, sometimes. Sometimes they just show a movie or something." She knows he doesn't mean the flippancy of that "something." But, still, these assaults at unguarded moments, none passes without exacting its toll.

"I better walk Romeo before it gets dark." Her dyspeptic fluff of a dog lies on a princely pillow. Such a seductive lassitude has taken hold of her in these high yellow rooms she fears she'll surrender her remaining time to watching clouds.

"Is it cold outside?' From the folded stack in the right-hand corner of her top dresser drawer, she takes an olive and gold scarf. Before she steps out, she will need to reassure herself in the foyer mirror that its stripes complement the persimmon of her jacket.

"A little ... maybe ... I don't know." The boy is massaging the sweet spot behind the dog's ears. Each of her children had Marvin's reddish hair and blue eyes, but in this boy, so caught in the long and painful birth of his manhood, she sees in his dark, sweeping brows the youthful beauty by which she survived.

◆ ◆ ◆

In the basement where they lived beneath their father's little dry goods shop Mina watched her little sister trying to wake him.

"Leave him, Sara."

"What?"

"Just leave him. We have to go." Their father sprawled across a sagging bed. The bed and a washstand were the only furniture on one side of miserable little space where they all slept. The room backed out of a hillside and had one window overlooking a narrow yard where noontime light washed a high plank fence. A blanket strung from a rope sliced the room lengthwise. Behind the blanket was the mattress where she, her sisters and brother slept.

"Mama's gone to the station?"

"One of them came," her younger sister said. "I think he had a dog. I don't know. I was under the mattress." Months earlier their mother had pulled up the floor under the mattress, burned the boards and hollowed out four body-length impressions in the dirt. At night Mina, Sara and Asher, their brother, and even little Leah, took the dirt and carefully spread it around the yard, one handful at a time. Mina always spread hers along the fence, pushing against the planks in the dark to see if they moved.

"When I came out, Mama and Leah were gone."

"Was Mama wearing her red kerchief?"

"I just told you, I didn't see them."

"What about Asher?"

"He's gone."

"To the station?"

"I don't know."

"How can you not know, Sara? I told you to watch him."

"I did watch him. I watched him leave. He just bolted. Mama couldn't stop him. I don't know if he was going to the station or what. Where are they taking us?"

All morning Mina had been trying for news, but no one had time. Even before they were at the station, details were snuffing out their lives: Levi Jacob wondering if he should take his violin or a sweater... Lili Sherer sewing family pictures into the lining of her coat. No one looking anyone in the eye. Things. They wanted things ... the smaller, the better. Soldiers were on every side street. She sneaked into the old bakery, climbed out the back, and over fences to get back to the basement room.

Mina pulled the blanket aside. On the mattress was a sock doll — Leah, their baby sister, had named it Bunny. Its head had been ripped open and stuffing spilled out. "Look at this. Look at what Papa did to Bunny. This is how he got the drink." Two days before, they had watched their mother sew her wedding ring into Bunny's head, but their father had been watching too.

"Come on, Sara, leave him. He'll be all right. He'll find a way. He always has." She watched her sister's eyes taking in the little room's details. The pathetic little washstand. The sorry blanket. How could poor Sara think they were worth remembering?

"Come on," she said again. "We have to go."

Echoes of abandonment fluttered over the cobblestones. An old man with a prayer shawl and a bleeding hand hobbled by. A buxom woman in a maroon beret struggled with a suitcase that wouldn't stay shut. Every half block, she'd have to stop, carefully fold its contents and struggle on. A young mother pushed a baby carriage with a little girl tagging along beside. The mother would halt, beat her to stop crying, then push faster—they had to be at the station by twelve. In Sara's eyes, Mina recognized that uncomprehending stare of their neighbors.

"Sara, you go. Find Mama."

"What?"

"Go to the station. Find Mama and Leah."

"Alone?"

"Just go."

"But what about you?"

"I can't leave him. I've got to try to get Papa." And almost believing it herself.

"How?"

"Who knows? Maybe Asher's come back. I'll do it. Go."

"I'll come."

"No. No. You go. Find Mama." She was already stepping back, willing Sara forward, and hearing that other voice, the one from a man who came into the shop almost every day even when there was nothing left on the shelves: "The last two boards of the fence, I'll loosen them. Get through. There's a space in the back of the coop. You can crawl in. Just you. Understand? Just you."

"Find Mama, Sara. Look for her red kerchief. Tell her I'm coming." And all the time, Mina was stepping back… stepping back … studying Sara's face. And then turning, running. And hearing Sara calling, "Mina!"

"What?"

"Bring Bunny."

"What?"

"Bring Bunny. Leah will want her."

"Just go, Sara."

✦ ✦ ✦

St. Bart's Way is narrow, and along its granite curbs the sycamores and maples have pried up the sidewalk. The trees hold a sort of primacy and for their sake, young parents, who themselves once tripped on the cantilevered walks, stoop to kiss the bloody knees of their own crying children.

The houses pass from one generation to the next as subtly as silver acquires patina. Mina's seen them at wide doors, sometimes with gray hair, sometimes with privileged-streaked blond, their eyes drinking in that part of themselves coming up a flagstone path—some sibling whose shoulders slant as theirs do, or whose head tilts to volleyed helloes. Even their clothes drape alike over mirrored bones—those at the door—those on the flagstones. This, Mina thinks, she will never know.

Women who would consider resetting their gems a first-order violation, think nothing of throwing their husbands' old golfing jackets, frayed as November leaves, over their shoulders to walk their dogs. Sometimes Mina wonders if any of them were customers of hers and Marvin's, if she was the one fitting skirts over their tummies, showing them the transformative powers of a neckline. What would she do then? Extend her hand? And say, "Why, Mrs. Crane, how good to see you. Mina Nagy. You remember from Nagy's Apparel. I never forgot that navy suit with the white piping. Yes, I'm living here now, with my son, Dr. Nagy." And all the time she'd be eyeing the old golfing jacket, remembering the sort of man who sold it, a man she and Marvin knew from the trade. A man smiling the smile only a man on commission can.

At the apex of the street's curve is a white house with four dormers punctuating its slate roof. Mina admires the symmetry of its Revolutionary icons—its weathervane, the garage cupola, the eagle knocker on its heavy door. Between the door's panels hangs a sheaf of red and gold corn. There are pumpkins on either end of the wide steps: the face of one scowls—that of the other grins. Such a strange American stew, she thinks, an all-but-forgotten Colonial past brewed with something more primal, unbridled.

An SUV turns the corner, passes her, then backs up. Rose lowers the window, "Do you want a ride home?"

"Romeo's not finished." The dog is questing for the perfect tree.

Rose says, "I bought some flounder for dinner." Every night she announces what they are having for dinner as if she needs Mina's permission. She should be beyond that, Mina thinks. "Sounds wonderful." Her daughter-in-law will have a cookbook on its clear plastic stand before she gets Romeo home.

When she opens the door, Rose doesn't smile at her, or coo to Romeo as she usually does. She's sloshing parsley in a small porcelain rinsing sink. Jason has told her about the assembly, Rose thinks. And when the boy goes to the refrigerator with his chastened walk, she's certain.

Rose waits until he leaves. "You don't have to go, Mina," she says. "Jason can explain. Let them get someone else. Or I can get Gary to tell them. It's just too much." She thrusts the parsley into a copper basket hanging from the sink's edge. The front of her slacks is splattered with water.

On the green marbled counter a TV is playing, and a man with close cropped hair and a flawless silk tie talks about public trust.

"It's all right," Mina says.

"You're going to do it?"

"Jason didn't know what he was asking. He didn't mean anything. I'm thinking about it." Under a swan-necked faucet Rose rinses translucent filets. They drape from her hands like swags of white damask. The question of whether Mina will go to the assembly hangs too; the two women cannot look each other in the eye. Where is justice, Mina wonders, if history intrudes on this earnest woman, her daughter-in-law, who lifts a colander as gracefully as Eve reaching for the apple.

She's afraid to look away from the man with his exquisite tie, talking about "right-thinking citizens." Afraid she'll see a curl of smoke snaking under the door, spilling over the harlequin tiled floor, and wrapping around her ankles.

The sun was high, and having no shadow, she felt invisible. She had the sense of running in a bubble. As though a benign gelatinous seal separated her from the cat lolling on a green bench, an old woman running with an empty basket.

When she turned the corner an arm grabbed her—he must have had a face—everyone has a face—but what she always will remember is that grip. "Where are you going?" She will never know how she thought of it, how she had the presence of mind to say, "Please, I'm unclean." Something in his eyes recoiled—he hadn't been prepared for that. "Please, I'm unclean—it came when I was at the station. I have to get a rag. Please, I need a rag. I'm unclean."

Even as he threw her down, she could see she had touched a nerve, had invoked something fearsome, something demanding acknowledgement. And when there were shots, he left off kicking her almost as if relieved. She stayed on the cobblestones until she couldn't hear his boots any more.

Their drygoods shop had been emptied long ago; no need to bother going there. Instead she went down the outside steps to the basement rooms where they lived, all the time, hearing in her head: "The last two boards of the fence, I'll loosen them. There's a space in the back of the coop. Just you. Understand?"

In the room with the window to the yard, their father's arm was flung over his eyes against the sunlight. When he groaned she knew he would waken soon. That's how it always went: first the roaring and the drunken beatings, then the sleep a step from death, and, finally, the painful wakening. "Papa," she said. But, if he awoke, what then? Staggering to the station? ... already late. Would he even go with her?

And then she noticed his feet: how could that be? He had had his shoes on, she was almost certain, when she left with Sara. He did have them, didn't he? But where were they? What had he done with them? And, then she realized... Asher! It had to be. Asher would do it—take their father's shoes. In a wink he would. Never think twice—his had always been the worst beatings.

And then she heard something ... or thought she heard ... what? A murmur? Something overhead? In the shop? "Papa?" He groaned. "Hush Papa." And there it was again ... now she was sure. A footstep, and another, now, upstairs. Whoever they were, they would have to go outside and down the steps: there were no inside stairs. Was there time to lift the mattress? Time to crawl under? Time to press her face into the dirt? And all the while hoping Bunny stayed where she was, in the middle of the brown stain on the mattress. So everything would look perfectly natural.

She never heard them come into the room. Just a shout and then the screaming; she thought it would never stop — she knew that sort of screaming — they all did — their father had taught it to them.

And then the shots. One. Then four into the mattress. She never forgot waiting to be dead. Never forgot thinking, *So, just your body goes. I am here. I am still here. Still me.* Never forgot waiting to float... out the window ... never imagining through the wall ... always out the window. Floating. Yes. She always thought of it as floating, not flying, but floating, high, so high, she would see the empty streets, the deserted houses, and, at the station, a red kerchief.

But, then, realizing she was alive and thinking suffocation was possible, she started to count to mark the hours. But she got confused and would have to start over, "One thousand one … one thousand two … one thousand three." She felt an urge to sleep, but would force herself: "One thousand one … one thousand two … one thousand three." How many seconds in an hour? Three hundred sixty? Three thousand, six hundred? How many times should she count? Darkness would be safest, she knew, but she had heard they always came back at night to catch the ones who had hid. "One thousand one… one thousand two … one thousand three…." She was on the fifth cycle when she felt she had to get out: if she didn't, her limbs would never move.

Her father was against the far wall, his legs splayed wide and the front of his pants bloodied. What they had cut off, was shoved in his mouth.

Even as she took the blanket from the rope she meant to cover him with it. But it was still with her when she climbed out the window, pushed aside the boards and crawled into the space behind the coop.

The salesgirl is a study in mahogany and gray, her only ornamentation the pearly beads tipping her braids. Mina appreciates her gabardine suit and black slides and the commiserative way their eyes meet in the dressing room mirror. When she holds a geometric scarf against Mina's suit, the salesgirl's brows arch in question. When Mina smiles, she whisks it off, saying, "I thought it was a keeper, too. Now, how about a half an inch off those sleeves?"

When the salesgirl asks, "What sort of a do are you ladies going to?" Mina's eyes cloud.

"We're just shopping. We might not be going anywhere," says Rose from the aisle between the cubicles. The jacket of her suit bunches over her backside. And the skirt is too short.

"You know," says the salesgirl, "we have pants that go with that jacket." Rose looks to Mina. "You'll probably get more wear out of pants," Mina says. When the saleslady brings them, they need shortening.

Mina studies the precise shade of cordovan in the thinnest line of her suit's plaid—there is just time to get a handbag. The one she wants must hold something larger than a handkerchief but smaller than her new scarf. If she goes to the assembly, it must open easily. She tries one, then another; Rose looks at none. Mina finally picks one with an envelope flap and slim straps and sees the tightness around Rose's mouth relax.

In the kitchen store Mina's feet have begun to hurt, but Rose's eyes alight from a white pitcher to a garlic press. "I want one of those things that separates pan drippings for Thanksgiving." When the clerk says they haven't come in yet, Rose selects a cheese grater. She tells Mina, "Gary thinks I'm crazy for grating my own cheese. But I tell him, it's the details that make a difference. 'After all,' I say, 'when you operate, you're just as proud of the closing stitches as you are of the valve job, aren't you?'"

This woman my son married, Mina thinks, she is so solid. In the food court she and Rose eat their yogurts near a fountain under a skylight. A half dozen youngsters mill at the fountain's edge. All their clothes, Mina thinks, look uncomfortable. The girls' navels show. And the crotch of the boys' shorts drip past their knees. All wear totemic jewelry. Mina thinks they have created themselves from plastic stones and metallic dyes. The girls have silver-toned mouths; the boys' heads have been tipped in gold.

"I hate that weepy bitch, Alison," says a girl with amethyst hair. "I gave her five hundred hits."

"She's just a filthy skank," says another, "but I only gave her two hundred. I gave the rest to Patrick. He makes me sick. I'm sick of looking at him." She wears a cross at her throat.

"They're talking about that TV show, *Popular,*" says Rose. "The one that follows six teenagers from around the country. Each week the audience gets to vote someone off the show. The one who's left gets a new car and a trust fund worth two million dollars."

"Patrick's a real suckass. I want him so gone," says a boy. "Christ, did you see him when he got his SAT scores. I thought he was going to bust a fuckin gut."

"I used to tease Jason that he should sign up for the show. If he got chosen and was the last one, he'd have two million dollars."

Mina doesn't tell Rose that the children at the fountain have mothers too, mothers who must love these offspring so bereft of promise. One with a tuft of hair under his lower lip lights a cigarette and the smoke drifts over Mina. When she looks at him, his apology is profuse. "I didn't mean to offend you," he says, flicking the cigarette into the fountain.

"Brandon!" the girl with the cross shrieks. "You asshole. You'll clog up everything." She starts to paw at the water, almost falling in. The boy starts to splash too. "Fuckin butt," he shouts, "Get up here. You get up here, you fuckin butt. You'll clog everything up." The others join in. Mina's getting wet. When she stands, the girl who started it, gushes, "Oooh, I'm so sorry." She starts to dab at Mina with a napkin. "Look, Brandon, the lady got all wet."

"All wet? Oh, my, that's so awful," he says. The others are closing in, dabbing too—"And it's such a pretty jacket. Where did you get it, Lady? J.C. Penney's? Sears? They've got such pretty stuff at Sears. Do you want us to send your pretty Sears jacket to the dry cleaners? My mother knows a real good dry cleaners." She hears their laughter, as if it came through cotton batting and when she looks up, the Jack o' lanterns on the banners lofting from the skylights grin down on her.

✦ ✦ ✦

She should have known he'd come, even though she had told him to stay away if it had snowed—they'd see his tracks.

"Mina," she heard him whisper.

Between the cracks in the coop, he was silhouetted against a ribbon of violet rising in the sky over the fence.

"Mina!" again.

"Asher, go away!" How he had known she was in the coop, he had never said. The first time he came she had asked him where he was hiding and he had only answered, "Not far." His visits were becoming more frequent, more reckless. The last time, he had begged for a chicken, but she hadn't dared. She knew he wouldn't leave. She rolled on her other side to the true back of the coop and with her fingertips counted the boards. When she pressed the fourth one, it sprang out—the man had made it so—she reached in and felt, first something moist and sticky, then, a peck and another. Then, something warm and ovoid. Two of them.

"Mina!"

"Wait! I have to put the board back."

She could scarcely see him, but could make out that his hand, when he took the first egg, was shaking. He tried to crack it against his teeth, and then against the edge of their father's shoe. When it spilled into the snow, he scooped both snow and egg into his mouth. Mina tried to pick up all the shell fragments before giving him the other—now a streak of pale yellow pushed against the violet. This time he managed to crack the egg against his teeth and arched his head back to swallow. When he dropped the shell, Mina saw it was smeared with the blood from his gums.

"Let me stay here with you."

"You can't, Asher." The light was growing; the rooster would crow soon.

"Come on. He only comes to you at night. I'll get out. He won't know."

"He'll know."

"Maybe I could give him something."

"What?"

"What you do. Maybe that's what he really wants."

"He's not like that."

"Oh no? What's he like, then?"

"You have to go, Asher." The rooster would start soon … at any minute the man would come for the eggs.

"Get me a chicken."

"I can't. His wife counts them." The rooster started. Her brother was backing away, still saying, "Get me a chicken, for God's sake, Mina. A chicken."

And she was saying, "Asher, wait," and getting, not a chicken, or even an egg, but the blanket. And now the crowing was continuous and he was going through the boards, and she was crawling into the space behind the coop just as the door to the house screeched on its hasp.

Through the cracks she saw the man stoop to examine the

bits of shell and watched him grind them into the snow. He studied the tracks to the fence, then made a business of fetching a hammer, then some nails, his boots obliterating the footprints. What she will remember is that the rhythms of rooster and hammer were only prelude to the beat of his belt against her back that night when he dragged her out, tied and gagged her, so that her screams were heard by her ears only. She will remember that for months she counted the chickens to keep from going mad, and the morning the rooster stepped on a chick before its second wing was free of the shell, and that the sun was so bright the morning the door to her space behind the coop opened, she couldn't see the faces of their former neighbors staring at her with every expression but sympathy.

In the mirror on the back of her closet door, she tries the scarf one way, then another. Too much flair, she'll appear frivolous; too little, tentative. She takes the scarf off, folds it in half, then slips the ends through the loop—give them flair.

She needs everything she can summon, plus all she's been given—her new handbag, the sunlight through the dormer windows, the yellow walls—she needs them to sustain her. She goes to her dresser, opens the bottom drawer, and takes out a tissue-swaddled shape. She places it beside her new bag and folds the paper away, first one raggedy leg, then another. Next a raggedy arm, then a second. Of course, there is no head. She touches the doll's wound softly, as if her finger could cauterize the gash. She, who's sewn countless hems, changed whole shoulders, this she never sewed. She taps the spilling stuffing back into the cavity—she will not mend it, but she will lose not one fiber more.

The yellow walls shimmer around her, and out the dormer

window the autumn morning sky and leaves are all dazzle and fire. Whatever purchase she has, is rooted in Bunny. She wonders if a headless doll is testimony enough, if it will teach privileged young men that their least evil act has consequence? That there's no such thing as a little evil? Can anything teach that?

She folds the tissue over the doll as tenderly as she once covered her sleeping babies with flannel blankets. Then slips it into her handbag and adjusts the handles over her shoulder —the bag hangs only as low as her breast, and she feels the soft lump of Bunny against her as she starts down the stairs. Gary and Jason are in the foyer.

"You look great, Grandma," the boy says. He's wearing a blazer with the school's crest on its pocket. She almost cannot bear the sweep of his brows.

Rose comes in from the kitchen. Her pants flap about her ankles; she's worn the wrong shoes for the new length. Still, it's she who hugs Mina. "You don't have to do this, Mina." Even now, she's saying, "We'll come up with something. A flu or something. Right, Gary?"

Mina looks at her family, backlit by October light through the fantail transom. What, she wonders, would command their energy at this moment if their history had been different? What would lay claim to their thoughts? Romeo's latest fit of dyspepsia? A new kitchen range? Tutors for Jason? Isn't the more worthy purpose to tell what she knows: that the eddies of evil are endless.

She checks herself in the mirror and looks back at her family. She wants to free them of the pain in their eyes, but knows that it's not herself who's caused it, but the convergence of memory and duty summoning them to this moment. "I have," she says, "done much harder things in my life."

BELLINI'S BRUSH

The evening air is clear and cool, and the water springtime blue. The pavilions around the Inner Harbor are a mid-Atlantic version of the arcade at St. Marco, and the tourists waddle with their French fries in a type of Baltimore *passegietta*. None of them notices the boat with luffing sails struggling against the wind. But I do.

With my mind flitting to my problem, then flitting away, I'm grateful for the distraction—the way the sun washes the boat's sails first pink, then white. When the wind socks them, they turn gray—unless you've sailed, you can't know what's at stake.

The summer before I met Ziggy, my mother decided that my sister and I should take boating lessons: Dad had a staff position at the hospital plus his private practice. We'd made the move to St. Bart's Way; my sister and I were in Briarley School—sailing seemed appropriate.

For the last lesson, Lizzie and I had to right a capsized boat. "Grab onto the keel and pull down. It will right itself," our instructor said. He was blond; he wore a Colgate T-shirt; for Jeff, I would have raised the Titanic. We'd hoist our chests onto the keel and then pull down, riding it under the water. As Lizzie and I sank, our bodies would float away from the hull and we'd lose leverage. We were teenagers; our hands weren't strong, so, before the boat was fully righted, our grips would slip. Like the dial of a compass, the sail would spring toward the bottom, and the boat would catapult Lizzie and me to the surface.

"Again," Jeff would say.

Who knows how many times we tried before a dangling line tangled Lizzie's ankle. I tried loosening it before I surfaced, screaming almost before my mouth was out of the water. Jeff dove and brought Lizzie up coughing and crying. That evening, when Mom set our certificates on the mantle, she said, "You could play lacrosse in the spring and sail in the summer, Melissa. I could ask your father to get you girls a little boat." Lizzie rolled her eyes and I said no. It's funny I should remember those lessons now.

I'd better start walking; Ziggy's never late. The wind is picking up, and I hunt in my bag for a hair scrunchy. I don't know why, but I feel as though I should look my best for him. My hair is probably my best feature, blond and curly—my mother used to call it "vibrant." My eyes are watering. And I know my nose is red and runny. Not a pretty picture to present to a man who's about to learn he may become a dad.

When I try catching my hair, my bag drops and my keys spill out. A woman in a pink windbreaker and frizzled hair picks them up, never letting go of the hand of a little girl wearing a jacket with a hood down its back. When she hands me the keys, I thank her, but it's like everything else in my life these days—awkward.

To be thirty-one and get caught like this. Ziggy is the best person I know, and if I say, "I'm preg," he'll be picking names before I get to "nant." If I don't tell him—if I just take care of it my own way—I know my secret would always be like that rope around Lizzie's ankle, tugging us down.

My sister's the only person I've told. The first thing she

said was, "Are you going to keep it?" More than anyone, Lizzie knows the consequences of whatever choice a woman makes. Until her junior year at Skidmore when she had an abortion, she fully expected to marry Peter Holgrum. "I never told Peter," she said. "But somehow it got between us. The saddest thing is, he never knew why I really broke it off."

Our mother had died by the time Lizzie got married to Andy Watts, so I had to play Wedding Prime Mover—dealing with the florist, the caterer, our father. After the rehearsal dinner, I was carrying a centerpiece out to the car, when, in the mirror over the bar, I saw Peter Holgrum, his shoulders wrapped around a beer.

I've taken three self-tests and gone to a doctor and still can't conjure BABY. Lizzie told me her Katie seemed real even before she was conceived, as if she and Andy had this dream of a child, and the dream was so powerful, it just had to become real. I know I really have only two choices: to marry Ziggy, or to not keep the baby. I'm not strong enough to go it solo—my roommate from Oberlin did that after we graduated. She went to law school, clerked for a federal judge, and raised her toddler alone; she'd call me at midnight, crying.

When the woman in the pink windbreaker pulls up the little girl's hood, I see it has teddy bear ears, and I wonder if that little girl, too, was a dream, and if all lucky babies first kick their heels in the Land-of-Their-Parents'-Dreams. I wish my baby were that lucky, but it just isn't. If I keep it, once it learns to calculate, it will know it was never a dream baby. Is that any way to go through life? I haven't felt so confused since my mother died.

Newspapers brought us together. Ziggy's father had the delivery route that included St. Bart's Way. After lacrosse, I'd be too tired for more than an hour or two of homework, so I'd wake up early and do more. Whenever I heard Mr.

Kadykowski's old station wagon coming down the street and the soft plop, plop of the paper on the walks, I knew I'd better make my crib for trig.

The morning the paper was supposed to have an article on Briarley School's undefeated lacrosse season, I wanted extra copies, so I threw a sweatshirt over my pajamas as soon as I heard that plop.

Who knows what Ziggy saw when his high beams hit the legs of my flimsy pajamas? He was driving for his father who'd fractured his wrist at a ballgame the night before — broken bones are one of the perils of alcoholism, but I'd learn that later.

When I asked him if he had any extras, he said no; he wouldn't know until he'd finished the route, and then he had to take his sister to school before getting there himself. But when I came home that afternoon there were three. Of course, Mom had gotten a half dozen, so Ziggy's didn't really matter.

"Some boy left those for you, Melissa," my father said. "He seemed nice enough."

Whenever Ziggy'd call, I'd troll for that cynicism I found so attractive in the boys Lizzie and I knew. Maybe cynicism wasn't taught at the Jesuit high school Ziggy went to. Then, maybe cynicism is a luxury when your father drives a paper route and your mother is a cafeteria worker. All I know is that he never let me joke my way around anything.

Instead, I got, "Well, Melissa, are you saying Portia is representational of all Renaissance woman, or is she a creature of Venice and its mercantilism?" Or, "Your thesis isn't really all that clear to me: is it that Venice venerated St. Mark because of his religious importance, or because of commercial benefit arising from an evangelist's relic?" And, too, he was possibly the ugliest boy I'd ever seen. When he asked me to his senior prom I said no—even Lizzie said I should have been ashamed of myself. When he went away to Boston College, I scarcely noticed.

He'd write sometimes and call. "That Ziggy fellow still around, Melissa?" my father would ask.

"He's going to get a master's degree—in health administration. Health administration!" I'd tell him. "That's his plan! He's probably going to work for an insurance company setting your rates. Did you hear me, Dad? Ziggy could be setting your rates!"

"Thank God someone with sense will be doing it," he said.

My phone is ringing, and even before I fish it from my bag, I know it's Heather, the intern at the Washington museum where I'm an assistant curator. Her ambition crackles over the shrieking gulls: I didn't leave out the latest draft of a catalogue for a Bellini exhibit we're having this fall.

"Melissa, I can't find it," she says. "It's not on your desk, like you said you'd leave it."

The wind has really picked up and I'm getting cold. I'm supposed to meet Ziggy in the café of a waterfront museum, but it's farther than I thought, and Heather is going on about how she's looked in my "in" box and under my Murano glass paperweight. She reminds me of myself — of the person I was before my mother died. "I wouldn't be bothering you, Melissa. I mean, I know you have something really important to take care of or you wouldn't have left early, but Bernice might be asking for it."

"I know where it is, Heather. I decided to take another look before passing it on."

"It's just that you said you wanted a second pair of eyes to see it before Bernice."

"It's six-thirty, Heather. Bernice has probably gone home."

"Actually no … for some reason she's still here."

The traffic is heavy and I can hardly hear her. A dark blue Volvo passes me, beeps, slows, then turns the corner. That's all

I need, some Volvo-driving ninny, stopping "just for a drink" before heading home to the wife and kiddies.

"Well, if Bernice wants to see the draft, Heather," I say, "just tell her I've locked it in my desk—that I wanted to take another look, okay?"

"That's what I should I tell her?—that you still want to look it over? Not that you want a second pair of eyes to see it?"

"Just tell her, she'll have it first thing in the morning." The Bellini exhibit is my idea. I've been wanting to do it since I went to Venice the summer after my mother died.

Her death was an accident. The March after I moved to Washington, my father was at a radiologists' conference in Chicago. The night he left, fog and a sudden temperature drop glazed Baltimore in black, invisible ice. Mom was wheeling out the trash when she fell on the driveway. Her head hit first. The garbage men found her.

By that July, I still couldn't come into my apartment without finding restiveness and sadness scrunched in my couch, munching their way through MTV. I called Ziggy, and he came down from Hartford where he worked for an insurance company.

At a five-stool shack on the Eastern Shore we bought hot dogs and ate them at a tippy table in the parking lot while the cattails whispered.

"What's awful," I said, "is that I can't get the irony out of my head." Ziggy shuddered away a yellow jacket. "That garbage men found her. Mom, with all her little pretensions … I was just beginning to understand them. What kind of a daughter sees her mother's death as ironic?"

"The truth is, Melissa, there is irony there. But that doesn't make your mother's death any less horrific." He didn't have acne any more, but his ears still stuck out.

When I swatted at the yellow jacket and spilled my coke,

he got me another. "Why don't you go to Venice, Melissa?" he said. "You've always wanted to."

I did, but it was a mistake. Venice is not a city you should see alone. The sheer improbability of it—you need someone to say "Yes, this is real." And, too, it was hot and crowded. I spent my time chasing Tintorettos and Titians and, then, two days before I left, came face to face with Giovanni Bellini. I'd studied him, of course, but there he was—in the flesh, so to speak, only five centuries late.

Giovanni Bellini bathed his figures in a peaceful, forgiving light. When I looked at his *Madonna and Child with Saints*, I felt that glow enveloping me. And I wasn't the only one. A long-limbed woman whose bottom had worn soft circles in her jeans was in the gallery, too. She stopped at the painting, and her hand touched her cheek as if it had been warmed by Bellini's brush. A man in a T-shirt with "It Must Be Found" on its back came in and took her other hand in his.

That was when I got the idea for the exhibit. "Am having a great time with a guy named Giovanni Bellini," I e-mailed Ziggy.

"Enjoy yourself," he mailed back. "P. S. They do teach art history at Boston College."

Two months ago, I was in New York making the final arrangements to ship Bellini's *St. Francis in the Desert* from the Frick. Ziggy met me. It was cold and rainy in Manhattan, and we slept together because there seemed to be nowhere else for "us" to go. But it was a mistake. In the morning, Ziggy could hardly look me in the eye. And now I have to tell him it is a mistake compounded. It would be better if I just got rid of it, now, before BABY becomes real.

It isn't fair to Ziggy. I need him, but I'm not in love with him. And no man should settle for a woman who needs him more than loves him. We're not a good match. He's so literal, and I'm only ever a word away from a double entendre. And, too, I had dreams of cobbled piazzas. And ageless art. No, I cannot do what my mother did: make a life out of holidays and birthdays strung like pearls. I know what it would be: Thanksgivings at Lizzie's house, Christmases at mine. Our kids at each other's birthdays. And Ziggy getting the candles I'd forgotten. And him saying my hair looks great when I know it doesn't. And my hearing him defending insurance companies to Andy Watts, and me suspecting he's only working for one because he has a family to support. No, this I cannot do. To myself. To him.

I turn around and start back toward the pavilions. The traffic is rushing toward me and the sidewalk is too narrow. I'm tired and cold: I have to get back to Washington, call Bernice, tell her I need a day or two off—I'll get her the proofs then do what I have to. If it costs me Ziggy, that will be just another loss to roll up with the others: my mother, my twenties, the girl I was.

A car is slowing. Its headlights are so bright, that I almost don't realize it's the blue Volvo. The driver lowers the window and says something. I ignore him: I don't even want to raise my eyes for a police car. The driver says something again. Then —I can't believe it—he's backing up against the traffic. I can't hear him for the horns until I make out Ziggy saying, "You're going the wrong way, Melissa."

On the rear passenger-side window is the outline from the new car sticker. I don't want to believe he bought a Volvo, the quintessential family car. I don't want to think that he knows and did the first, most responsible thing he could think of. I don't want to look in the back—there might be a "Baby On Board" sign. I get in and say, "I'm preg."

"I know."

"How?"

"Later," he says and drives into a neighborhood of former shipyard workers' homes with pitted aluminum doors and formstone facades. Through the lace curtains, I see televisions flickering. A door opens and a teenager hunches his shoulders against the wind. Who knows if he's going to the local bar or around the corner to his grandmother's? Ziggy pulls up to a tattered little park where some kids are still swinging at balls in the spring twilight.

"How did you know?" I ask.

"That night, in New York, you slept right away, but I just couldn't. So I just watched you. Your hand was clutching the pillow ... holding on so tight."

"You watched my hand? That's how you knew? You went out and bought a Volvo because you watched my hand?"

"I bought the car when you called. But I knew before that ...your hand, it was holding on so tight, and then, it just relaxed."

"That's it? My hand let go?"

"No. More like you were hanging on for dear life. And then, just like that, you didn't have to anymore. The next morning you had this glow. You were so bright I could hardly look at you."

Nothing is this simple, I know. Nothing.

But, then, what if it is? Dear God, what if it is?

FIREWALKER

———————— ◆ ————————

Alone in her daughter's latest apartment without even her needlepoint for distraction, Marian wandered amid two sleeping hounds and the chaos of cartons. Youngish—Marian thought—Sara is youngish for the apartment's style—probably fifteen years younger than the other residents. Oh, Marian knew them, those well-boned Baltimore women with jawlines surrendering to chocolate, like the definition of the crown moldings beneath coats of China White semi-gloss.

Sara would be the first of the next generation—the whirligigs. Plants and dogs and incidental furniture cobbled together. How far could she possibly have gone for dog food and coffee?

Sara's paintings peeped from between the cartons; it seemed to Marian that her daughter's pictures were always stacked like that. As if they weren't worthy of the wall's permanence. Marian remembered visiting her in Boulder and hearing her ask the hirsute musician she lived with then— "Help me get a few hung. Just a few." It never happened. They leaned against the walls like children whose benighted parents have brought them to a cocktail party. Small, reverential landscapes, tender still lives. More joyful than beautiful. A penchant for siennas, ochers and, almost always, a touch of crimson. But the artist's brush was tentative, as if she were afraid to commit her hand to what her eye knew was true.

When she first moved back East, Sara worked as a research librarian at Bowdoin and had grown enough as an artist so the faculty included her work in a student exhibition. Marian had insisted on traveling to Maine for the opening—Edmund was in the early stages then and the trip would distract him Marian hoped. But, of course, it didn't. Marian pictured him, one of three men bothering with a tie, holding a plastic cup of ginger ale as elegantly as his favorite baccarat tumbler. For Edmund, the exhibit was but another ordeal among decades of Sara-ordeals. By their daughter, he did his duty, nothing more.

And now Sara was back in Baltimore. Marian imagined her in a heavy Peruvian sweater hurrying to the university library, burying herself in the stacks, surfacing in the twilight to walk her dogs. On weekends going to openings of other people's exhibits. Perhaps another lover.

In the quiet of the apartment, Marian felt the carapace of her forty-year deception cracking. Forty years of deceit and duty, surely that had been atonement enough. She would do it—tell Sara the truth about her blood and bones. The truth would either destroy her or free her to trust the surety of her eye.

Edmund had been dead three years now, and their sons, they would reel, but not break. They had too much at stake—Matthew practicing law in Connecticut—Frank, two children and on the tenure track. Besides, their sons were too tightly woven on Edmund's warp. If she told Sara who her real father was, perhaps she'd leave life's periphery for its center.

At a stirring in the hallway, Harvey, the retriever, looked to the door. Max, a pound dog, cowered, expecting the worst. When Sara opened it, he jumped up and slobbered joy all over her cheek. She set the dog food on the floor and crouched to him, the scuffed leather sack she used as a handbag slipping from her shoulder. "Are you my goodie boy, Maxie? Are you my goodie, goodie boy?" Her long fingers stroking him, she smiled at Marian: "Sorry it took so long, Mom. The damn ATM was out. If we're going to eat, you'll have to pay. I'm starved."

The diner, with its mulligan-stew menu of the owner's native Indian tastes and American carbo-cuisine, was pure Sara. Aromas of tandori chicken entwined with the smell of sputtering cheeseburgers. "Nice, Huh?" Sara grinned. She could always do that—find humor in the offbeat, as if she had sucked at the teat of the inside joke.

"Different." Marian smiled, watching Sara's hair cascade about her face—that hair—Marian alone in a hospital and cupping a tiny girl's skull and weeping to hold her lover's most obvious patrimony—a jubilation of red hair.

After two blond, straight-haired boys, here came this little girl with her tangle of red curls. At first, Marian tried keeping it cropped close, then straightening it in braids. One of Edmund's sisters or his brother would recall a great aunt with red hair and then there was that second cousin on their mother's side, wasn't there? Marian had dug in the attic for albums until she found pictures of a distant red-headed great uncle. These almost forgotten relatives, how she blessed them for giving credence to the story they all needed to believe, that curly red genes had survived the generational slurry to surface in this little girl.

And then there was that artist's eye. A week before her fifth birthday, Sara pushed her peas around her plate, eyed the blond brother to her left, the blond brother to her right, and announced, "The only thing I want for my birthday is a big box of paints. I'm an artist!" At the party, Edmund couldn't bring himself to say, "Make a wish, Sara."

✦ ✦ ✦

She smiled, now, at the purple-haired waitress—Marian watched her taking in every detail, the multiple earrings, the aborigine nails—that wonderful intensity as she discussed the merits of gucchi abu over lamb vindaloo. In Sara's world there were no strata: as a child she had chatted to Marian's maids as cheerfully as she did with Edmund's partners. In Sara's world all tables were round; all diners, equal.

Greta Conyers, Marian's friend, retired like herself from the Briarley School, had said it best at a luncheon two weeks earlier—Greta's own daughter, living in Wyoming, her emails full of wolves and bears. "They're always starting over," Greta had said. "Perpetual sophomores. Familiar enough to be comfortable, uncommitted enough to get an anticipatory thrill. No permanence, only possibilities. Forever young."

"What are you thinking about, Mom?"

"Nothing. I should get the house painted."

"Frank said you were thinking of selling it."

"That's your brother's idea. I don't know. It needs to be painted."

"So you're not going to sell?"

"Greta Conyers is in Long Acre Heights. Do you remember her? We go to lunch. It's a retirement community in Worthington Valley."

"Then it must be hell. That witch couldn't live any other place but. Of course I remember her. She flunked me in trig."

"It's probably too late to get it painted now, but I should at least get the walk fixed before winter. The flagstones are very loose."

"I always liked the flagstones. Their colors. Especially when it rained."

"It needs work."

"How Dad hated shoveling them, remember? I thought he was going to burst a goddamn blood vessel."

"They're really coming up now. Especially near the oak tree," Marian said.

"He'd get so red in the face. Christ!"

I have to tell her," Marian thought. Her life has become a whirlwind, cycling from coast to coast. She'll never find terra firma, will always be fighting Edmund, not knowing his is the wrong ghost.

She remembered him—scarf hanging from his neck, top coat open, grim faced at the snow shovel, and his daughter, her red hair atangle, calling, "Daddy! Daddy! You'll get your feet wet!" And his mouth tightening as the flagstones snagged the shovel. And his, the only shovel scraping on St Bart's Way. He had a meeting—always a meeting. And the walk had to be cleared; someone could slip. "They could break a leg, understand, Marian?" And she, watching him go, his the first tracks down St. Bart's Way.

"You OK, Mom? Want a taste of my Channa Masala?"

"I'm fine. This lamb is actually better than I expected. "

"This diner reminds me of a place I stopped at in New Mexico with Kyle. You remember Kyle, don't you?"

Marian vaguely recalled a bearded, balding counselor, something with drug abusers.

"It was in Las Cruces. A German place that sold Mexican food. I swear they sold hasenpfeffer tortillas. The maître d' wore a serape and lederhosen. I swear."

Even as she talked, Marian watched her eyes follow the back of a forty-something, his gangly wrists protruding from his corduroy jacket, his head bent in the stoop of the self-involved intellectual. The sort of man she was always bringing home. The sort who'd expound on some theory of literary criticism while Edmund listened, bemused, asking a question at the appropriate time so he wouldn't have to talk, while Sara sat enthralled.

"Something wrong, Mom?"

"I'm all right. Do you know what Greta says is the worst thing about those retirement communities?"

"I suspect for Greta the worst thing is wherever she happens to be at the moment."

"It's the lights. Greta's something of an insomniac. She corrected her papers at four in the morning. Can you believe that? Well, now she wakes up even earlier. The worst thing, she says, is looking out the window and seeing those flashing lights. Then you know that someone else is gone. She thinks the management has the ambulances come at night so the residents won't get upset. She's probably right."

"I told you, Mom. Greta always was a bitch. The next time you want someone to go out to lunch with, call me. Not her."

Marian recoiled. She had seen them—the aging daughters taking care of aging parents, toddling them to the beauty shop, the dentist. Their own gray hair needing a touch-up as they beeped open their vans for their mothers. She didn't want to become just another distraction so Sara wouldn't notice her own shadow lengthening.

The wind caught them as soon as they left the diner. Marian watched Sara search for her keys in her handbag.

"Before you take me home, take me to Keswick Road. The thirty-three hundred block."

"Why?"

"Just something."

She thought she'd have known the house right off, but she had to retrace her steps; it had been "rehabbed." In a brave effort to add elegance, urban homesteaders had painted the red bricks beige and hung a door with mullioned panes in place of the aluminum one Marian remembered. There had been a flight of narrow stairs to the second-floor apartment and she had given each step a name: Alexandros, Aeneas—the last—Richard. She heard Sara behind her but didn't turn.

"Mother, what are we doing here?"

"Nothing. I just wanted ... Nothing."

"Why are we here?"

"I grew up here."

Alarm widened her daughter's eyes. She thinks I'm cracking up, Marian thought.

"Oh, Mother, no! You didn't grow up here. On Winslow Street. You remember. You grew up on Winslow Street," her voice oozing that coaxing tone Marian thought would be appropriate soon enough. "We have to go now, Mom. I've got to go."

The door opened. A young woman with sun-streaked hair and an oversized man's shirt came onto the porch. She held the door ajar as if listening for something. "Can I help you?"

"No. No thank you; we have to go," Sara said.

A toddler stepped onto the porch and wrapped an arm around his mother's leg. He grinned at the two woman on the walk. Marian took a step toward the open door; she felt the press of Sara's arm.

"I grew up here. I wanted to come here again."

"Do you want to see it? The house?" The young woman had the sort of trusting nature founded on blond-streaked privilege.

"No ... no thank you. It looks as though you've got your hands full. Thank you for asking." Marian felt Sara's hand on her arm until they reached the Toyota. The October wind was whipping that red hair—streaks of gray. "You grew up on Winslow Street, Mom. Got it? Winslow Street!"

Maybe she should stop here. She had lived one lie so long, why not live another—let Sara think she was slipping, losing her grip. What was to be gained from the truth but pain?

After all, that was what Richard had been all about, after Edmund's slavish belief in the idea of marriage as enterprise: the marking of milestones, desire deferred in the hope of greater fulfillment. So she had fled to Richard and discovered the exquisite pain of the firewalker; the pain of pleasure without promise. "I grew up the first time on Winslow Street."

"What do you mean 'the first time'? You only get to grow up once."

"You only get to be a child once, Sara. You get to grow up many times."

"So, what's this place?"

"This is where I grew up after Winslow Street. With someone else."

"What are you talking about? Who?"

"Someone. An artist." Richard. His name was Richard.

"Who?"

"I dropped a book. He picked it up." When he stooped she had known there were no accidents, only fate beginning millennia before, aiming like a meteor to the afternoon a book slips from your grasp, and a man bends, exposing the glory of his hair to the sun through mullioned windows of a school where he's come to meet his sister Greta. And then he's standing over you—yourself being tall, but he taller still—and saying to you, "You know, dropping the *Iliad* won't free the world of wooden horses." And then you climbing the stairs ... Alexandros . . Aeneas. And anticipation moistening even your palms. And all moments you're together are liquid and, being liquid, transient, until made solid in a baby you name Sara.

"Who? Who are you talking about, Mom?"

"Someone I met. It was at Briarley. He picked up a book. I had dropped it."

"What are you telling me?"

"I think you know."

"You were already married when you began teaching at Briarley."

"Very."

"Jesus, Mother. I don't need to know this. I just don't need to know this!" The wind was whipping her hair. "Having an affair is your idea of growing up?"

"I didn't mean that. I grew up later."

"Will you stop talking in fucking riddles?

"I grew up when I left him."

"Jesus! I don't need this! You and your riddles. I don't need this." She was fumbling for her keys, getting into her car, her hair in her eyes, and then driving away, leaving Marian alone, watching the ratty Toyota going away, watching her daughter going away. Again.

Across the street the second story windows of the mean little row houses were opaque in the afternoon light, but Marian knew what they shielded. Those afternoons with Richard were spent in a room with identical windows—they had laughed when they rattled. She knew even now the wind was seeping across the sills, stirring all the loves, dreams, needs, disappointments, recriminations, and fears where they had lain for years under radiators, dressers and beds. All those incorporeal engines whirling now over the worn carpets, the dime store throw rugs, the wind blowing them down the hallway where they would shelter in the corners of the stairs until the wind caught them again and swirled them to the lower hall —its floor smoothed by years of skips, steps and staggers. And then the wind pulling them under the door with its frosted glass and down the concrete steps to the walk slicing the little yard. And there they were free to rise.

The red Toyota careened around the corner—Marian had known it would; the circles of Sara's peregrinations had grown tighter; she was too close to the center now to resist its pull.

She leaned across and yanked open the door. "Get in, Mother. I don't want a scene, but believe me I'll make one. Now get in."

Marian felt she had lost all volition; that she was alive only in her senses, the smell of dog, the crack in the dashboard, the can rattling somewhere in the back. Marian thought, this must be what dementia is like—to live only in your senses. My God! What a gift! She watched Sara, her hunched shoulders, her fingers wrapped around the wheel, her nails digging into her palms. Maybe keeping the forty-year lie was best. Was there such a thing as too much truth, she wondered. She had told Sara the easiest half and that had nearly destroyed her. Surely the rest would be too much.

But wasn't that how it had always been with Sara? Always someone, even her brothers, protecting her. Always someone thinking she hadn't the strength, without even giving her the opportunity to prove otherwise. Surely her endless peregrinations, and those rootless lovers came about because that's all they had ever expected of her.

"I can't face St. Bart's Way now, you understand I'm sure, Mother. You can call a cab when we get to my apartment. I just want to get home."

The neighborhood of sorrowful windows gave way to one with wide doors, chrysanthemums in riot. Sara shifted the Toyota with a vengeance.

"What I loved was the way you said it. So cryptic. So fucking ladylike. My generation, we're not so clever. We just call it 'screwing around,' Mother. The cruder among my generation call it 'fucking around.' But, as I say, they're so crude, those crude ones. You know them, Mother. The ones you would never let us play with, because, God knows, they were crude and we, God knows, were from fucking St. Bart's Way."

They had stopped at a light. A woman with long legs in blue tights pushed a stroller. A preschooler clung to the stroller's handle; in his free hand he carried a cluster of red maple leaves as proudly as a battle banner.

Marian wished she could take it back. What a vainglorious mistake she had made. Forty years she had held it secret and now this. She felt sick.

"My God, mother. Who was he?"

"No one. I shouldn't have said anything. I don't know. I shouldn't have said anything."

"What I want to know is why now? Why did you want me to know?"

"Nothing. I shouldn't have said anything." But she saw it was too late. Sara stared at her: "You said he was an artist."

"Did I?"

"Don't start with your fucking riddles. You know you did."

"His name was Richard Conyers. Greta's brother."

"That witch." The light changed. Cars were honking, but Sara didn't move. Marian watched her slowly realizing the enormity of the truth. Forty years hidden and here, at this corner, before this stoplight, everything, finally and forever, converging.

"He was an artist?"

"He was in Baltimore for a while, then moved to New York. I never saw him again."

"Greta had red hair."

"Yes. It's gray now. His was red too."

"Like mine?"

"Exactly."

The light changed again. Drivers behind them swerved around the Toyota. Marian concentrated on the crack in the dashboard. If one of her grandchildren were there, they would make a game of it, imagining it was the entrance to a magic cavern. She was a loving grandmother. They couldn't take that from her. She'd tried to be a caring parent. Some would say, even a devoted wife. None of it mattered: not the nursing, not the coaxing, not the encouraging, not the sustaining. Forty years. In the space of red to green, all gone.

"When I became pregnant, well, I didn't know for certain. But, then, when I saw you, well, there was no doubt."

"And Dad, or should I call him Edmund?—he knew?"

"I don't know. He never said anything."

"Well, that must have just been fucking peachy. You didn't say anything. He didn't say anything. We were all just one big peachy goddamn happy family on St. Bart's Way. You, me, Edmund, Matthew, Frank. A veritable fucking Brady Bunch."

Sara threw the car into first. Marian watched the flickering reflections in the side mirror. The cars behind. A blue SUV with a white haired woman in a baseball cap. A truck with a ladder on top and a man eating a sandwich. Then the bridge over Stoney Run. Lamps. So many times over Stoney Run. Did it always have lamps on the balustrades?

Marian wanted to sink into the anonymity of the civic river. Politeness would suffice. She studied the reflections in the mirror, the apartments, the unlikely deli, the blazing Bradford pear trees. Then Sara stopped.

"There's a phone in the lobby, Mom. You shouldn't have any trouble getting a cab. You'll understand if I don't ask you to come up." And then she was gone. Her red hair thrashing in the wind, her sack of a bag slipping from her shoulder.

Marian called a cab and didn't notice the teasing wind as she waited. The apartments on either side of the street grew dark in each other's shadows, making the street a gusty canyon. And then, suddenly, Sara was upon her again. "He knew."

"What?"

"He knew."

"Who?"

"Edmund, for Chrissake. The man you were married to. He knew."

"What do you mean?"

"Since this is such a fine day for truth saying, try this one on: your husband knew all the while that you had been fucking around. Oh, excuse me, 'had an affair.' There, does that make it clear to you? Your husband knew. He knew all along."

"How do you know?"

"Because he told me. That's how, Mother."

"What?" Marian shielded her eyes from the wind and looked for the cab.

"Up in Maine. He told me."

"Maine?"

"Yes. Maine. You remember. The exhibit. Or are all your memories only of yourself?"

Marian saw a flash of yellow turn the corner.

"What did he say?"

"Right when you were getting ready to leave. You were in the ladies' room. He said that I should keep painting. He said, 'You've inherited a good eye.' 'Inherited,' that's the word he used. And you know Edmund always chose his words carefully.'"

And then Marian slamming the door, saying "Take me to St Bart's Way," and seeing Sara hunched, running away, struggling against the wind.

She had an urge to move; she told the cabbie to stop a block from her house. It had been years since she, who had once pushed a baby carriage on every block, walked down St. Bart's Way. Marian remembered a little red-headed girl looking at the leaves of a maple tree and crowing, "Yeyyow! Yeyyow! I love yeyyow, Mommy!" And Marian's grip tightening on the stroller handle, her little girl's delight in color, her uncanny eye, making her own back stiffen.

That memory was more real than the wind snipping now at her coat. Or the leaves in the ivy beds, where a young father would have his children, on a November Saturday morning, clean them away. His rake, as Edmund's had, snagging on the ivy roots, and the leaves, the sycamore's indistinguishable from the oak's, all of them equally reluctant to surface.

She wondered what had it had been based on—that presumption of righteousness underlying all that endeavor, all that effort, even raking leaves. As though back-bending work undertaken on a chilly Saturday had greater moral content than the same work done by the transient men who shuffled up the street on weekdays. As though they could forestall whatever was coming. Squirrels, thought Marian, we lived like squirrels and their crazy hoarding. What did we think we were holding off? Only with Richard had she found neither compromise nor promise.

Once she had known every neighbor on St. Bart's Way. The Hearns—Ed dead of cirrhosis twenty years now, Joan in Arizona with their daughter, or maybe Nevada; the Kanes—six? seven? years in Florida, no card last Christmas. And now she couldn't even connect the houses with the cars. The young family next door, three children like her own, but now the father's gone: three brave pumpkins on the porch. A divorcee just moved in across the street; her children visited on weekends. What would she think if Marian rang her bell, brought her a basket of welcome? Did anyone do that sort of thing anymore?

At her house the wind had whipped the leaves into the borders of the flagstone walk buckled at a treacherous slant from the pressure of the oak tree's roots. She remembered

Edmund saying "Sooner or later, they'll have to be replaced, Marian. It's either the walk or the tree. You'll have to decide" —she in heels, the black sheath Edmund liked, he holding her elbow—always the best of manners—to yet another dinner party. But the afternoon she walked away from Richard had sapped any strength for decision. And, in the end, she never did choose between the stones or the tree; they both lasted longer than Edmund.

Still, had Sara been right? Had Edmund known all along and said nothing? Did his duty? And did it until the effort sucked the life from him, and he was left holding a plastic cup and looking at paintings evidencing another man's talent in the hand of a daughter he had raised. And was that, too, not love?

Mail littered the blue Tabriz in the foyer: bills, advertisements—she didn't even recognize the name of the stores—a postcard showing lost children, a solicitation from Briarley School. She picked up a flyer from K-Mart. It was addressed to "resident." They got it right, Marian thought. That's me. I'm resident. Stooped on the rug, she ran her thumb over and over "resident," as if a caress could summon meaning, any meaning.

PRIME MERIDIAN

Heaven forfend that one should consider Wilcox Miller a violent man. *Au contraire* ... our Wilcox is but the most prudent of men. The most deliberate. The most highly regarded.

The very model of rectitude, our Wilcox is esteemed beyond estimation. Why, aside from that little deal he concocted with his neighbor, Henry Cottman, some thirty years ago nary a fly speck has sullied his reputation.

And that? What was that? That little deal? What, after all, was poor Wilcox to do?—he and Margaret with three children in private schools, the oldest about to graduate. And one didn't send one's son to Pelham Hall and then pack him off to a state university ... did one? Of course not. Wilcox, a Princeton man himself, knew which way doors swing. So, if he and Cottman cooked up their little deal and then cooked the books, what of it? Who was hurt? The IRS? Pshaw!

No. No. Aside from that trifling matter, our boy Wilcox has been beyond reproach. Retired now, he volunteers at the Episcopal soup kitchen, donates as generously as anyone can reasonably be expected to. Even serves on a commission or two ... the Committee for a Greener Downtown ... that sort of thing.

Moreover, he's made every effort to keep up. No slipping into that boob tube stupor for him.

Last January, in fact, he bought a telescope. Keen on seeing what heaven was all about, he'd told Margaret. Set it up in that little alcove off the bedroom … tried to be quiet while Margaret slumbered with her book over her bosom.

When spring came, he'd told her, "The vernal equinox is coming. I have to get the precise moment. The precise second when the heavens are in balance." The equinox. The very acme of alignment. To see that, well, that would be something.

So, you see, there has to be perfectly reasonable explanation why our boy stopped still as a stone in the middle of a hospital hallway and contemplated whapping his old neighbor with an eight iron. There had to be a perfectly sound reason for him to consider, some would say anticipate even, slicing a bloody divot from Henry Cottman's skull.

There our boy Wilcox was, halfway to the elevator bank, his new golfing sweater comfortable and loose on his shoulders, and bloody mayhem and certain murder in his heart.

Just moments before, he had watched his former neighbor's toothless mouth dilating to an ever widening omega, when, from the subterranean fermentation of Henry Cottman's mind, gurgled an astonishing apology: "I'm so sorry about Margaret. I'm so sorry about your Margaret." Like some homeward bound spirit it wafted—and, then, silence, leaving our poor Wilcox staring at Henry's omega twitching at phantom dreams.

At first, Wilcox had thought the utterance merely a natural effusion of poor Henry's moldering marrow. And blending, as it did, with the fundamental rhythms of end-stage life — inhalations, exhalations, the drabby drone of motors and burbling oxygen tanks—Wilcox had just let "So sorry about Margaret" swirl away.

Besides, he wanted to get home. Get some lunch. Get his telescope ready. Maybe get out that book on medieval meridians Margaret had found for him.

Still, it deviled him all the way to the elevators—"So sorry about Margaret. So sorry about Margaret." He'd pushed the "down" button three times before it hit him. Of course! Of course! A deathbed confession. Out of that gaping omega had gurgled a confession! Of course! What else could it mean? "I'm so sorry about Margaret" … it had to be! The old coot had swived his Margaret! Niggled her. Maybe been niggling her for years! What else could it mean? The old fart! The unmitigated profligate. The out-and-out son of a bitch. Oh, Wilcox would whap him. Whap him good. Swive his Margaret, would he?

But then our boy realized his eight iron was in his car. Besides, it was brand new. No. No. Not the eight iron. Not his spanking new eight iron.

Better try something else. Pull the plug! Trite, but, what the hell? Its triteness was its very virtue—who would think anyone would be so unimaginative as to pull the plug!

"Pull the plug! Pull the plug!" A body heard it all the time. Wilcox had just used it himself, just the other week, when their youngest came for another "loan."

Everyone must be doing it. Oh, yes, he might be a Johnny-come-lately to this murder and mayhem business, but he would do it right! Back to the bedside! Back to the bedside!

But what was this! A vision of lush, feminine symmetry blinded him. Like two perfect scoops of French vanilla ice cream a pair of delectable buttocks in creamy linen slacks bent over Henry's bed. Veritable Gemini mounds, they were so perfectly pulchritudinous only God's own compass could have traced them.

Blinded by the sight of their dazzling roundness, the murderous thoughts buzzing like hornets in Wilcox's brain demurred and silently folded their wings.

The woman straightened up and tossed Wilcox a casual, "Oh, Mr. Miller, hi." Something about that laser smile was familiar ... before, when it had worn braces, Wilcox had seen it in his rearview mirror. He'd be driving their daughter Alice to school ... and ... yes ...yes ... Meredith Cottman! He'd forgotten Alice's little friend, Meredith Cottman, Henry's little girl. How the two of them, Alice and Meredith, would giggle as he drove them in the morning.

"Well, Meredith, well, hello. I ... well, I didn't know anyone was here. I must have missed you in the hallway."

"Oh, I take stairs whenever I can. To stay in shape, you know. I was just saying 'Hello' to Dad ... he likes it when I whisper in his ear."

"And I've just come to say one more good-bye," said Wilcox.

The machines were droning, calling him to yank their plugs. But here this woman was. With her mounds, no less. What was a poor man to do?

"Oh, I think Dad is so lucky to have a friend like you. You and Mrs. Miller, you were our best neighbors. How is she?"

"Who?"

"Mrs. Miller ... your wife." When Meredith Cottman took her sunglasses from the top of her head, a perfect curtain of blond cascaded down. And when she stuck the glasses' earpiece into the V-neck of her T-shirt, well, that was perfect too. Damn!

"Oh, she's fine ... keeping busy ... committees, gardening, that sort of thing."

Meredith Cottman took her father's hand, and an Elysian dream must have tickled Henry, his omega twitched so. How

94

could that miserable perfidious scoundrel have fathered something so lovely? Moreover, how could he have fathered someone who loved him back? No ... no ... let the poor girl be alone with her father. It was the only decent thing. Manly, really.

The son of a bitch would probably be dead by Thursday anyway.

The tableau—the beautiful young woman holding her father's hand—that fortunate ear piece looped in her neckline—they couldn't lull the hornets forever. And by the time Wilcox had turned onto St. Bart's Way they were abuzz again. Whipsawing their shriveled little antennae. Rubbing their desiccated little legs against each other. Disgusting.

Wilcox frosted two slices of bread with mayonnaise and sandwiched a mountain of ham between them. Margaret was gone to that committee of hers. At least she said she was. For all he knew she could be cavorting with every Tom, Dick and Harry in town. Well, let her! At least he had his peace and quiet. No one to nag him about him about his cholesterol now. He'd eat what he damned well pleased! Let her gallivant. Disport herself like a bedizened runabout. The wanton hussy.

Here he'd done the decent thing—cut short his morning golf, gone to visit a sick old neighbor, and what did he get for it? Betrayal and heartache. A man can only take so much.

On the counter, near a vase of daffodils, lay his copy of *Meridians of the Old World.* He'd wanted the book for years. And here Margaret had gone, just the other day, and gotten it. Said she found it while looking for children's books for that tutoring center she said she volunteered in. She hadn't so much as looked up from the flowers she was fixing."Look what I found," she'd said to him. As if she didn't know how he'd hunted for it in second-hand shops whenever they were off on one of those trips people take at their age.

She never so much as gave him a sidelong glance, just kept

at her flowers to a fare-thee-well. He tried explaining meridians to her. How essential they were to measuring Earth's cycle. How critical for knowing when the equinox would be—the only way one could get a grip on time, really.

Suddenly she had held out her hand. "A ladybug!" she'd said. Here he'd been explaining how the universe worked, and she was at the sink, fussing over a bug.

"I wonder what her sense of time is," Margaret had said.

"What?"

"I wonder what her sense of time is. This ladybug's." She'd reached to fill the vase, pivoting on her heel in that way she had.

"What are you talking about?"

"Say this ladybug is crawling up an iris leaf. I mean if you measure time by measuring distance, isn't a ladybug's sense of time different from ours? I mean her sense of distance is, so why not her sense of time?" Oh, she could always do that to him: shanghai some thought. Just as he was making her see how things work. How everything works, really.

There, in that kitchen, as familiar to him as the feel of his whiskers in the morning, Wilcox had been struck mute by this woman who pivoted on her heel from counter to sink, whose hands cupped petals away from the rush of water sluicing from the tap. Just as thirty years earlier he'd be downstairs and hear her singing to their youngest, "Itsy Bitsy Spider." And, yes, his eyes would water. And he couldn't speak for the fullness of his heart at that contralto of hers.

He ate his sandwich and thumbed through *Old World Meridians*. But he found it dry and didactic. When he got to the balderdash on the grid intersects being energy focal points, he threw it across the kitchen. He didn't feel the least bit guilt-ridden when Leonardo, their basset hound, skulked toward the hall, careful to not let his nails click, click, click on the kitchen tiles. Let him go. The lop-eared cur.

✦ ✦ ✦

"Cuckold ...Cuckold." Wilcox could hear the gravel in the Cottmans' old driveway chiding his every footfall. Oh, he'd get to the bottom of "So sorry about Margaret" if it killed him. He'd gone up into that alcove off their bedroom and tried to set up his telescope but couldn't concentrate. Every time he'd adjust the eyepiece for the equinox, or attempt to get a bearing, there was Cottman's old house. He'd never decode the true meaning of "So sorry" until he saw his own house as Cottman had.

The alcove was where Margaret used to sew. From across the street, Cottman must have seen her signal—Wilcox was sure of it—that had to be how they concocted their filthy little scheme—they'd signaled with the lamp. He'd come up the stairs and she'd be sewing some dress for Alice—they had three kids in private schools, every penny counted—and he'd find she'd moved the lamp. No telephone calls. No notes. Just moved the lamp. That had to be it—lamp right: "Wilcox is home with the flu." Lamp left: "Wilcox will be in Wilmington tomorrow." Perfidious. He could imagine them chortling under the sheets: "Pulled one over on old Wilcox!" And all the time, him sweating the details of that deal he'd concocted with Cottman.

Nothing to do but bamboozle his way into Cottman's old house. It wouldn't be hard. Pajama people lived there now—wore nightclothes morning, noon and night. Margaret said they were Indian, a couple of doctors, ophthalmologists. "Lovely people" she said. All his knew is that they weren't smart enough to know that pajamas didn't cut it on St. Bart's Way.

"Cuckold. Cuckold." The stones mocked his every step.

He was almost at the door. The only one home during the day was the husband's doddering maharaja of a father. How hard could it be to bamboozle someone like that? And, of course, there was the woman Wilcox assumed was the housekeeper. When, suddenly—what was that?—for every "Cuckold" of his, Wilcox heard a "Cuckold" reply. How could that be?—a double cuckold! My God! A pricksong cuckold! No … no … not a pricksong cuckold! Please, not a pricksong cuckold! A man could only take so much. Wilcox whirled around and, there, two steps back, grinning like a turbaned elf was the old maharaja. Every other finger had a gaudy-stoned ring, and his right hand held a cocktail glass with a slice of lime doing a shimmy around an ice cube.

"Well, here you are, neighbor. I was hoping you'd grace us with your presence sooner or later. So good of you to come over."

"I'm sorry to bother you," said Wilcox, "but I was wondering if you could let me use your phone. Ours seems to be out."

"Well, of course, good chap. Out? … you say your phone is out? Oh, my, that is a bother, isn't it? Your cell, too?"

"What?"

"Your cell? Your cell out, too?"

Did the old coot think Wilcox was the sort who used those ridiculous little pieces of plastic he saw everyone screaming into?—the conversations he'd been forced to overhear.

"Well, actually… ."

"Oh, no matter … no matter. I don't like them much, either." The old man ushered Wilcox into the house. "Winifred! Winifred," he called, "we've got company! Fix another Gift of the Raj, my dear, if you would." A young black woman in a yellow dress stuck her head out of the kitchen. "Another Gift of the Raj coming right up." She smiled at Wilcox and he thought it wasn't his cup of tea to be chummy with a house-keeper, but if that was what the old maharaja wanted, it was no business of his.

The lime danced around the cubes in the old maharaja's drink. "Well, actually make it two, dear. I'm running a little flat." Wilcox thought he heard a wink in the old man's voice when he said Winifred was his "assistant," all the while leading Wilcox to the sunroom and saying how he and Winifred started their cocktails early—they had to settle in before "Oprah." And, of course, Wilcox would have to join them. At least have one Gift of the Raj after he finished with the phone company.

"No ... no ... I don't want to intrude," said Wilcox. "I ... I...." He couldn't think of a polite way to say watching "Oprah,"—well, he just wasn't that sort.

"Oh, I know what you're going to say," the doddering Ma-haraja said, "that you wouldn't be caught dead watching 'Oprah.' Well, Winifred and I don't really *watch* her, either. It's more like we *steal* from her." The Winifred woman came with the drinks.

"We'll be across the hall," the old maharaja said. "The phone's on that bamboo thing my daughter-in-law got. She thought it would remind me of the old country. Fat chance." He put his hand on the Winifred woman's back. "Well, come along, my dear. We mustn't miss our gal."

They were nearly out of the room when Wilcox realized he hadn't introduced himself. "By the way, I'm Wilcox Miller."

"Oh, I know ... Margaret's husband. A lovely woman ... trades recipes with my daughter-in-law. Smashing woman! Simply smashing!"

All about Wilcox were thingamajigs and whatnots begging

a body to peek inside. God knows what might slither out of that basket in the corner. And those itsy bitsy boxes—probably full of seeds. Oh, he knew how that went. You planted them. Then you smoked them. These people, they were famous for that sort of thing.

Worst was the painting of the kohl-eyed princeling over the couch. Positively treacle-eyed, as though he were inviting Wilcox into some cosmic joke.

No ... no ... Wilcox told himself, don't get inveigled. Don't get ensnarled in something you can't get yourself out of. Just get to the bottom of "I'm so sorry about Margaret" and get out. Skedaddle. That was best.

He picked up the phone—but whom to call? Still, he had to call someone—that doddering maharaja and his "assistant" might be listening. He couldn't call the phone company and say his phone was working fine. No ... no ... that would be crazy. He looked at the smiling princeling: no... no ... there was enough craziness to go around.

Wilcox dialed home and got Margaret's voice on the machine. "It's good to hear from you, and we're so sorry we missed your call. Let us make amends: leave a message, and we'll get right back." Damn that contralto of hers.

Wilcox took a long swallow of his Gift of the Raj. "Margaret ... Margaret, I'll see you when I get home."

When he hung up, he was no closer to the truth than when he first heard "So sorry about Margaret" gurgling from Henry's omega that morning.

Wilcox went across the hall to where the TV was playing and sat down—he didn't want to leave his Gift of the Raj half finished. The old maharaja and his assistant were scribbling on yellow legal pads. He gave a course at the community college, he told Wilcox.

"Strictly non-credit, you understand. All women. Not one

male in the whole class. Talk-show victims, each and every one. What can I say? So, I take something from 'Oprah' and cast it through a tantric prism. Makes it seem familiar to them, but not quite. They eat it up." The show was on its third commercial break, he said, and he and Winifred still had no slant for that night's lecture.

Wilcox thought the two of them were getting a little desperate—not that it was any business of his.

The couch was cushy: Wilcox's knees were almost to his chest, cutting off his air. He felt his head getting light. He felt himself sinking to a slough of confusion. The Gift of the Raj cast everything in a downy light, but it couldn't quite drown out the hornets' buzz—"So sorry about Margaret." Wilcox felt like someone mesmerized by an approaching tsunami. Too enthralled to save himself.

He willed himself to shut out the TV—some fool was nattering on about how much happier we'd all be if we'd just "open our eyes to what is before us"—and set his mind to hatching a plan to get upstairs, see his house from Cottman's perspective, and get out. Margaret moving the lamp, well, that was just a theory. But if Cottman had a clear view of that little alcove, well, the theory just might hold water.

The old maharaja was getting peevish—no theme for the night's lecture was forthcoming. He was getting positively irksome. Just to placate him Wilcox blurted, "How about 'Seeing with Surprise Eyes'? Use that for tonight's lecture: 'Surprise Eyes'."

The old maharaja sprang from his La-Z-Boy. "By God, that's it—'Surprise Eyes'—that's it, My God, Wilcox, you're brilliant. Top drawer! Oh, they'll eat it up. Saved my life. Yes sir! I'll just mix it up with some Vedantic voodoo ... serve them a real mulligatawny. A real pastiche!

"I'd love to throw in a little relativity theory, some cosmology, but what can I say? … these ladies … no … no … mustn't confuse them. Give them something almost familiar. Not quite, but almost. They'll think I'm a Goddamn mystic. Yes, sir!"

As the old boy went on, Wilcox felt his mind wrap itself around a plan for getting upstairs.

When the Winifred woman went to get more drinks, Wilcox followed her into the hallway. Years ago, he told her, when he'd come to fetch Alice from playing with Meredith Cottman, Henry's wife had opened the door. She had held her finger to her lips signaling Wilcox to be quiet and then led him to the staircase. From some room above floated the voices of his daughter and Meredith Cottman singing something about "I Honestly Love You." Their song was so sweet, he'd almost wept. The tender adolescent longing of it. The sweet harmonics.

Wilcox could see the Winifred woman had a good heart. A man has a sense for these things. He was just about to tell her he wanted to see the room where his daughter had sung, when the words stuck in his craw.

Instead, something implacable and brutal, burbled out: "I think my wife cheated on me." It just rose up, like a poison he had to regurgitate—"I think my wife cheated on me." No preliminary. No prelude. Just that god-awful irrevocable statement. Final. And beyond retraction.

"What did you say?" the Winifred woman said.

Again: "I think my wife cheated on me."

"Margaret? Your wife? Why would you say such a thing?"

"I don't know. I think it was with Henry Cottman. He used to live here."

"And you're just worrying yourself about it now? I mean Dr. Malhortra has lived here six years."

"Well, I just found out about it." Wilcox felt awkward and

ashamed: here he was unburdening himself to her, someone he'd met only an hour ago. Someone who surely had troubles of her own. Still, the torrent of his confusion was unstoppable. "I went to see him in the hospital and something he said made me think it."

"Think it?"

"Yes, think it."

"But you're not certain?"

"Not really." She was staring at him as if she were weighing whether she could trust him with her thoughts. But he was desperate for whatever she could offer, and wasn't embarrassed to let her see it.

"What should I do?" Wilcox said.

"Well, sometimes we find trouble if we look for it," she said. "And sometimes what we see depends on how we look at it."

"What?"

"Like when we watch TV. Sometimes what we see depends on how we look at it. Like 'Oprah'."

" 'Oprah'?"

"Yes. It seems like the show's happening right then. While we're watching it. But it's not: it's taped. The studio is already dark and empty when we see it. Sometimes I watch the audience and think, that one, she may have gone home, taken a test and found out she's going to have a baby. Or, that other one, the one who looks so lonely, maybe she got on the train to go home and met someone. Just like that. It all depends. Sometimes we don't know exactly what we're seeing. Or what we know, for that matter."

Wilcox knew she'd let him go upstairs if he wanted to, but somehow he didn't have the heart for it. He listened for the hornets' buzz, but heard only a snore.

"I have to go," he said. "Say good-bye to the old boy for me. I hope his class goes all right." And then, "He's lucky you're his assistant"—he didn't know where that burbled from either.

The Winifred woman stood at the door. "Oh, I'm not really his assistant; I'm his nurse. His son felt he needed someone. We just call me an 'assistant' so he accepts me. And we don't even really go to a college—you see what he is. I just take him to my church. The ladies there have a prayer meeting every Wednesday. They're good about listening to him and that mumbo-jumbo of his." She closed the door, and when Wilcox started down the walk, the stones were silent. The door opened again: "Say hello to Margaret for us," the Winifred woman said and closed the door again.

Spring—always a splendid time on St. Bart's Way—the way the daffodils come, then the tulips. And the azaleas! Just radiant! Almost gaudy. It could overwhelm a body, if you weren't careful.

Thank God for evening. The way it softened outlines, muted shades down a tad. Count on evening to put everything in a better light. Not so harsh.

Wilcox stood in the middle of the road and realized he was famished. What a day it had been! He'd never forget it. Here he'd expected to play a little golf, visit a sick old neighbor, and fiddle with his telescope so he could catch the equinox. The irony of it: here the heavens were in equipoise. But everything down below was just plumb haywire.

Who could have imagined it, much less explain it. Henry's gurgling omega. The mounds of Meredith. An afternoon with pajama people. He'd been battered from pillar to post, no doubt about it. But, still, he'd never forget it. What a day.

And here, he was, in the middle of his street, the road just curving away to dusk. A woman with a little dog was coming down the walk of that house with the yellow door, and somewhere, a kid was bouncing a basketball off a backboard.

Wilcox opened his back door and smelled shrimp and butter. Margaret was at the stove.

"Where were you?" she said. "I thought you'd be upstairs with your telescope."

Wilcox didn't know where to start. He opened a bottle of wine and poured two glasses. She was wearing a large white shirt over green slacks. That she still could summon the panache to turn up her collar touched him.

"I found that book I got you—the one on meridians—on the floor. Isn't that strange?"

"Maybe Leonardo did it."

"Have you been reading about meridians, Leonardo?" she asked. She was a tall woman and wore her hair up in a series of combs. The light over the stove caught the blue stones of her earrings. Damn, but she was fine. Proportionate and fine. And that contralto voice of hers. She went to the sink and over the rush of water, he heard her say that their daughter Alice had called.

Wilcox sipped his wine and let the aromas of shrimp and butter entwine on the back of his tongue. Margaret pivoted back to the stove, and a curlicue of hair escaped a comb and rested behind her ear. Wilcox wanted to look through it—to stand behind her, close one eye and with the other squint through his wife's hair—and see what? Everything around him was so familiar he could find it blindfolded at midnight. The pepper mill. The sugar bowl. But, still, to see them through Margaret's hair, that would be something. Really something.

He went to her and put his arms around her waist. He watched her hands stirring. How plump and strong they were. How dear the faint spots speckling the joints between her thumb and index finger. He wanted to take them, turn them over, kiss her palms. She squirmed a little. "Don't forget, you've got the equinox tonight," she said.

He thought of telling her that those who go to bed early, get to stay up late. But he thought that might sound crude and Wilcox wouldn't want that. Oh no, no, not our boy. Heaven forfend.

ABIDING BLUE VELVET

———◆———

Just as had been predicted, almost on the stroke of noon, great feathery flakes began swooning among the glass towers and granite office buildings of downtown Baltimore. Their size and lackadaisical descent signaled a negligible accumulation — a nuisance, really, rather than something magical.

But, still! Snow! On Christmas Eve!

On the fifteenth floor of the Bartlett Building, a sense of surfeit flowed from the reception desk to the conference room with its foil-wrapped poinsettias and paper plates of sprinkled cookies.

"White Christmas ... White Christmas ... goodbye ... merry ... merry." In his corner office, Deke Sutton listened to the snippets of departure. He could imagine the paralegals and associates checking their pockets one last time for their bonuses before putting on their gloves. Deke, too, had a sense that they all shared something no less important for being unspoken. In the closing doors and exclamations, he heard the startled realization that Christmas had, indeed, come around again.

Surprising that it was here so soon. Astonishing, really. That four seasons had passed. Just like that. He shoved his hands deeper into his pockets and moved away from the window. Let the others hurry home.

Two weeks earlier, right after they'd sent their compliments to Juan for the crab cakes at their regular Tuesday lunch, he'd told his older brother Whit, "Good-byes are something I've never been very good at. But now I find that I'm not even good at hellos. I don't even want to bother with them. With the hope that 'hellos' carry. I don't have the energy for them."

The only sounds had been the snap of fresh cloths over the tables and the clink of dinnerware glasses being set lip-to-linen by men in white jackets. Out the window, the harbor's horizon was drizzling away to gray.

"I guess that means you won't be bringing anyone to Christmas Eve," Whit had said. "I think we'd better go to a restaurant this year."

"I'm not seeing anyone, if that's what you mean. But I don't just feel this way around women. I even find it's getting harder to be decent to ... well ... to just be decent. Just civil."

Thank God, he'd stopped short of telling Whit maybe he was out of sorts because he'd spent the morning with the divorce papers of one of their Pelham Academy friends—Whit's own separation from Betsy still was so fresh their three children winced at loud noises.

"I wouldn't worry about it. It's this holiday crap," Whit had said. "I have the kids for Christmas Eve. I have to have them to Betsy's parents' by nine on Christmas morning ... it's in the agreement. Leave it to the MacCauliffs to throw a real pity party for them. That's why a restaurant might be best for us for Christmas Eve."

Deke said he'd make the reservations.

"And can you get Aunt Elsbeth? God knows if Betsy will have the kids ready on time. If you can get Elsbeth that will help."

Deke had kept his questions about how Betsy was holding up to himself. Whit, well, he could be sarcastic, and Deke just hadn't felt like hearing that. He just said he'd get their great-aunt, buttoned the middle button of his suit coat and took out his credit card—it was his turn.

The snow was sticking on Charles Street and traffic was snarled. The leave-takings were growing fainter; things would be quiet. He could get a lot done. The thought crossed his mind that maybe he should go to his apartment before getting Elsbeth, but the Armbruster case, that deal with the Watermann contract, they were piling up. Better to work.

"Will you be needing anything, Mr. Sutton?" His secretary stood in the doorway. She's already halfway to picking up her little girls at her mother's, Deke thought.

"Thanks, Donna. I'm fine. I guess almost everyone has left."

"Just Meredith. But I think she'll be going soon, too."

"Who?"

"Miss Cottman. The paralegal in trusts ... you know." Deke remembered something at the partners' meeting. The woman's father had died sometime near Thanksgiving; there had been discussion of the size of the wreath. The other men referred to the Cottman woman as "Her Blondness," but Deke had stuck to his rule: aside from his secretary, courtesy titles always for the women at the office.

"Oh. Well, I'm fine. Merry Christmas, Donna."

"Same to you, Mr. Sutton. Sure you don't need anything?"

"No. No. I'm fine. Just, well, ... that little gift shop in the lobby, is it still open, do you think?"

"Carl's? Probably. People always need last-minute things."

"I thought I'd surprise my aunt, my great-aunt, really. You know how it is." No sense explaining anything more. Elsbeth was so private, living in an African violet world with her books and her dog. You don't expose someone like that to your secretary, have her spread what you told her all over the office.

He told Donna it looked like the snow was sticking; she took the hint.

When he'd mentioned to Elsbeth they'd be going to a restaurant for Christmas Eve, she had said, "Well, of course, that makes perfect sense. After all, Whit, well, he's got his worries right now. You and I, Deke, we've always been the flexible ones. You know, they've put the tree up in the lobby already. I took Lotte Lenya for her walk, and there was Dawson, wrestling it in."

Pure Elsbeth, Deke had thought, knitting the details of life together, binding her year-to-year. Nothing escaped her: the dogwood across from the Presbyterian church, the praying mantis that scared her dog, the cheese man at the farmers' market. So frail, she seemed almost incorporeal, almost as if she materialized out of blue air for holidays, weddings and funerals. Every family event, there she was—always cheerful, always thankful for whatever crab dip or chocolate-crowned cookie came her way. Even Whit's kids loved her.

But, still, Deke had surprised himself, telling Donna he wanted to get her a gift—he'd never done that before. What do you get someone like Elsbeth? And, too, she was old. To be eighty-something, alone, and still excited about a Christmas tree. How much of her enthusiasm, he wondered, was artifice, that ingrained graciousness, honed during years of private schools and Bryn Mawr teas. A friendliness she summoned to make you feel at ease, to give you something to chat about before you drove her home and she rode the elevator to her waiting dog.

Deke took out the files on the Watermann contract. Increasingly, details, not rainmaking, had become his forte. At the last partners' meeting, Old Man Carter had called him a tailor for the way he sewed up loopholes. Still, he was having trouble.

The facts kept escaping. Like quicksilver, he'd gather them up only to have them slip away. Again and again, he tried assembling them into a bastion of purpose, but they kept eluding him. And those he did grasp, seemed petty beyond redemption. Just to hear something, he made his chair squeak

Ten minutes later, he walked down the corridor to Old Man's Carter's office, making certain to jangle the change in his pocket—he didn't want to startle the Cottman woman. In her doorway, he cleared his throat, and she lifted her curtain of blond.

"I'm going downstairs, he said. "I just want you to know that you'll be up here alone." He didn't want to call her "Miss Cottman." They were the last ones—they shared that common denominator; there had to be some intimacy in that. And, too, "Miss Cottman," that sounded so stodgy; he was only forty-four, after all.

"Melody, is it?"

"It's Meredith, Mr. Sutton. My name is Meredith. But, I'm just about done. I just have to print out, and I'll be done."

"Well, I just wanted you to know that you were going to be alone, that's all."

"I won't be long. Mr. Carter needs this the twenty-sixth. I just need to print."

"Well, Merry Christmas."

"Thank you, Mr. Sutton. And you too."

Before the elevator doors closed he heard her printer beep. The gift shop seemed dedicated to the sort of doodads that women give each other to gush over and then put beside their computers. Nothing for a woman like Elsbeth, his grandmother's never-married sister. To be that old and alone: What would a woman that age want with brass worry balls? Or a pink padful of inspirational messages?

"Just a last-minute thing," he said to the black man behind the counter. The fellow wore a Santa hat over yellow hair; he didn't even try to hide his swish when he walked.

"I've been selling a lot of 'last-minute'," he said. He was eating chocolates. Deke fingered an angel with a pearl blue glaze.

Santaman said, "Those are popular."

Deke put his hand in his pocket. Even after she'd retired, Elsbeth had traveled with her Briarley School colleagues: the ruins of Petra, the coast of Patagonia, Singapore. Her apartment was a symphony of mementoes. Not to mention the things she'd inherited: the chests, highboys, sideboards, and Chinese porcelain some relative or other had collected.

The afternoon Deke had come to "fetch" her to the christening of Whit and Betsy's younger boy, the woman he had been seeing then had remarked about a bowl with an oxblood glaze.

"It's the workmanship that matters," Elsbeth had said. "That and the idea of connection fascinates me. Somewhere in seventeenth century China, someone made this. And here we are, you and I, on a beautiful Sunday in September in Baltimore, admiring it. Maybe your fingers are in the exact place his were as if he'd been handing it to you all this time." The memory of Elsbeth saying that was more vivid than the one of the woman's kiss.

"I just need something for my great-aunt," he said. "She's on in years. She doesn't need anything, really."

"We should all be so lucky." Santaman said. He popped a candy into his mouth then motioned for Deke to take one— the caramel had glued his mouth shut. He signaled he'd be back and went into the storeroom. When he came out, he was holding a red umbrella studded with white hearts. With a flick of his wrist, it whooshed open.

"Here, take it," Santaman said. "It's incredibly light. That counts when you're old. Does she still go out, your aunt?"

"Well, concerts. That sort of thing."

"There you go. It's really a Valentine's item, but in my boat, hearts go any time."

Deke took it. It really was light. He held it over his head, and then out in front to inspect the ribs; it seemed well-made. He snapped it shut, and there, in the lobby, was Meredith Cottman waving goodbye to Santaman. And there he was, a partner in the firm, holding that girly umbrella. He weighed her smile—it wasn't mean—and watched her duck into the snow.

"She's a doll, that one," Santaman said. "Right up to the time her father passed, she'd come in, get some little thing for him. I knew what she was going through—I went through it with my dearest friend."

Deke paid for the umbrella, went back to the office and tried to work. But the quiet was oppressive and he was getting hungry. He thought of those cookies in the conference room, but they had looked pretty pathetic. Store-bought, too. Stew, that would be good.

He went to that place those Koreans ran near the courthouse, but it was closed, so he had to go back to Charles Street. And, of course, all the sidewalks were covered. Who would shovel on Christmas Eve? He was almost at the Washington Monument before he found a five-stool place still open.

When he asked for stew, the woman behind the counter never put down her cell phone; she just couched it against her shoulder when she opened a can. Deke didn't say anything. The dinky plastic spoon she gave him felt so insubstantial that, with his eyes closed, he wouldn't have been able to tell if he grasped it or not. Touch, he thought, we don't appreciate the sense of touch enough. He looked around for someone to talk to, maybe something about which of the five senses was the most valuable, but the man two stools away had shaking hands and an untied shoe. The other one hummed every time he took a bite.

Deke ate his stew and tried to remember what he had done the Christmas before. Whit and Betsy had still been together, but the tension between them had been so thick he almost felt stifled by it before he rang their bell. And neither the MacCauliffs nor Elsbeth could dispel it. He'd been glad the woman he was seeing then had gone home to Miami.

Still, they had gotten through it: his niece Emily had shown him her new flute, and Betsy had surprised everyone by digging out the old one she had from when she played in the Briarley School ensemble. She and Emily had played "Greensleeves," and by the time dinner was served, Whit had mellowed enough to make his grace at least sound heartfelt. And Elsbeth, of course, had told her famous story about the time the Christmas the lights went out. How there had been a terrible ice storm when she and her sister were little girls, and how, just as Christmas dinner was about to be served, the lights failed.

"Well, don't you know, your grandmother and I, we had gotten the most beautiful sweaters that year: mine was trimmed with blue velvet and hers with grosgrain ribbon," she had said. "Well, the lights were out and Mother had guests up one end of the table and down the other. Of course, we had candles, so it wasn't a total catastrophe, but poor Cook, I don't think she had more than a word or two of English, and there she was struggling to get the dinner out. And the kitchen— well, candles are grand for dining, but not for serving. Oh, Cook, she was having a time of it, so Mother told your grandmother and me to help her. Well, it was pitch dark, I tell you, and all of sudden I didn't see your grandmother anywhere. Not in the dining room. Not in the kitchen. Not in the pantry. And, then, there she was, as helpful as could be, carrying out one platter after another. Of course, eventually the lights came on, and Mother had Cook serve dessert in the parlor, and there, under the tree, someone had switched our sweaters. Near your grandmother's presents was the blue velvet one, and near mine, the grosgrain. I tell you, I was about to throw a fit, but, Mother just hugged me to her and whispered I was not to dare make a fuss. Not in front of guests. So, of course, I didn't, but ever since then, sometimes I find it hard to abide blue velvet."

He remembered how Whit and Betsy's kids had listened; he knew they'd hear Elsbeth's story again in the restaurant this year. When he paid for his stew and stepped into the snow, the outlines of the buildings had become blurred, and the deepening twilight had given a purple cast to the Christmas lights streaming from the Washington Monument. He checked his watch: still over an hour before he had to get Elsbeth. A drink —rubbing elbows, shooting the breeze—that would put him in the Christmas spirit. He found a place down on St. Paul Street, but it was chockablock with people fifteen or more years younger than he was. A group in the corner was singing a beery "White Christmas" and when they got to "like the ones I used to know," they shouted it like drunken frat boys. What could puppies like that know about "used to know"? Their mocking, ironic tone irked him—they didn't even know how to drink.

A blonde girl had her back to him, and when she turned, he saw it was Meredith Cottman. A young fellow, a clerk for one of the judges, Deke thought, had his arm around her shoulder and was running his fingers through her hair. She smiled, but turned her head away. The fellow took his hand down, but she still reached for her coat. By the time the group had broken into another chorus of "White Christmas," she was walking toward the door. Smiling, but, still, leaving.

Deke held the door for her and turned up his collar against the snow.

She looked up at him. "Oh, Mr. Sutton. It's you."

"I thought it was you .... It's Meredith, right? Did I get it right, this time?"

"Yes ... it's Meredith."

"Let me walk you to your car."

"I'm, fine, really. You don't have to do that. My friends, you know, they mean well ... they've been telling me to get out ... now that my dad's gone. They all say that's what I should do. But, I don't know." Her eyes showed him the depth of her loss.

The snow crunched under their feet and fell on her hair.

"You really don't have to walk me to my car, Mr. Sutton. I'm fine, really," she said.

He wanted to tell her not to call him "Mr. Sutton," but felt now wasn't the time. He could see the snow was getting on her shoes: her feet had to be cold. He tore open the box with Elsbeth's umbrella—he'd tell his aunt he'd had to walk someone from the office to her car. Elsbeth was from the era of the courtly gesture. She'd understand.

Across the street, a car beeped when the Cottman woman pressed her key. Deke held the umbrella over her, but there was water in the gutter, and he had to take her elbow to help her over. Even through his glove, her coat, and who knows what else she wore, he felt the aliveness of her breast. The malleable quickness of it. How lush. How blessedly soft. Just a momentary thing. But, still, there it was. So warm.

And then he moved his hand lower on her arm, and by the

time they'd crossed the street, the sensation was only a memory imprinted on the back of his hand.

"Could you please wait a minute?" she asked. "I want to check my trunk. This time of year, well, people get desperate; I don't want to pull up at my brother's and find out that I've been robbed. I'm the high aunty, you know. I'm the aunty who gets to sit by the fireplace and drink eggnog."

Deke knew she was being effusive because of the drink. He wanted to kiss her and knew she'd probably let him. But he didn't want any kiss he gave her lumped with every other casual holiday kiss she'd ever been given—she had looked him in the eye, showed him something of her grief—you don't take advantage of someone like that.

In the trunk, tied with a bright red bow, was a babydoll carriage.

"It was too big to wrap with paper," Meredith said. "My niece is only three. It's not politically correct, I know. My sister-in-law will probably have a fit. She and my brother just moved back here from Houston. She's a microbiologist. She even has her own lab. And here I am, giving her little girl a doll carriage. I probably should have gotten a microscope, but this doll carriage was so cute. My niece is only three."

"I'm sure she'll love it," said Deke.

"I loved mine. I remember pushing it up and down St. Bart's Way."

He wanted to tell her how Betsy had taken Emily's picture the year she had gotten her carriage. And how Whit had put the dog in it, and the pooch had stayed while Emily pushed. He wanted to tell that story, but Meredith's feet were getting wet. When she got into her car, Deke noticed little collars of snow circling her high heels, and he was glad he hadn't given her a cheap kiss.

Then she pulled away. And Deke watched her go. And felt what he was. A man holding an umbrella. Alone. On an empty downtown street.

✦ ✦ ✦

He gauged the snow on the canopy of Elsbeth's apartment house; it had to be at least six inches. It was getting down the collar of his coat, but he didn't want to put up the umbrella. Using Elsbeth's gift for Meredith Cottman, that was one thing, but using someone's gift for yourself, that was another.

When he got to Elsbeth's floor, her dog began barking even before he rang the bell. And when Elsbeth opened her door she had to struggle to keep the creature inside.

"Lotte. Lotte, you Lotte Lenya, you be a good girl." His great-aunt's speckled hand reached for him. "Come in, Deke. Come in."

He stamped his feet just to make certain all the snow was off. On a round table was a little Christmas tree, and white candles and greens were on the mantle. Somewhere a radio was playing.

"Can you believe it?" Elsbeth said. "I can't remember the last time it snowed on Christmas Eve. I looked back in all my diaries to 1965 and couldn't find it. I'm certain I would have written it down, whenever it was. Come in. Come see. Come see how it looks from up here."

She seemed even frailer than she had at Thanksgiving—the way her eyes swam behind her lenses—and that sibilance of hers—the whole impression was one of spittle and bone. One of her hips had cantilevered higher than the other, and a slice of white slip flashed whenever she took a step. Deke knew she'd be embarrassed for it to be seen in public, but couldn't think of how to tell her.

"Come see, Deke," she said. "Come see." The dog picked

up a lime green rubber pig. "Oh, Lotte, Lotte Lenya, Deke doesn't want to play now. Just be a good dog." She went over to a bank of windows overlooking the rooftops of the houses just across Charles Street, every one of them plumb and four square, built to withstand whatever came its way.

In high school Deke had loved a girl who lived in one with east and west-facing sunrooms, a slate roof and flagstone patio. He remembered how, his junior year, it had taken him all fall to get the courage to ask his great-aunt if she taught a girl named Betsy MacCauliff. And how, a week later, Whit had stood in his doorway, saying, "Some girl named Betsy has asked me to the Snowflake Fling at Briarley. I guess I'll go."

He stood at Elsbeth's window and tried to pick out the MacCauliffs' house. How could he not know which one he used to drive by—used to make up some excuse, some other Briarley girl beside him, just to pass by where Betsy lived?

"Isn't it magical?" Elsbeth was saying. "Have you ever seen anything like it? So peaceful! We're so lucky!"

Deke looked down on her. At the bravery of her lipstick.

"I brought you an umbrella, Elsbeth," he said. "It had been wrapped, but one of the women from the office, well, I had to walk her to her car—her feet were getting wet, so I kept her head dry—that doesn't make any sense, I guess."

"Sense? … sense … ? Oh, Deke, I gave up on sense a long time ago." She held the umbrella over her shoulder.

The evening he had stood on the landing of the MacCauliffs' stairs and toasted Betsy's engagement to Whit, everyone but Elsbeth had smiled and smiled up at him, but from behind his great-aunt's glasses he caught sympathy. Later, Mr. Mac-Cauliff had cornered him in the kitchen, shook his hand, and told him it had been a terrific toast. Deke had been answering that a toast for your brother and his fiancée, well, that's something you want to get just right, when Elsbeth came out of the powder room. She was feeling a bit "peakish," she said. Would Deke walk her home?—Her apartment was only a block away. It had been a cool June and the azaleas were still in bloom. She had been what?—nearly seventy, when she astonished him by taking long, playful strides, like in that child's game—step on a crack and break your mother's back.

"This is how you do it, Deke," she had said. "Just one foot in front of the other. One step at a time. You get through it. You find joys the others are too busy to notice." He had walked back to the MacCauliffs' remembering the story his grandmother had told him of how she had given herself three weeks to steal the only boy who ever came calling on Elsbeth. She'd done it in two! He had considered taking his own long strides, playing the game. But he hadn't.

"We'd better get going, Elsbeth," he said. "Our reservation is at seven-thirty."

"Just let me get my coat and shut off the radio." Lotte Lenya picked up her pig and trotted after her.

He was left alone to look for the house where the girl he had loved had lived. Whit and Betsy, he thought—they had staked so much—marshaled three children as a bulwark against being alone. But still, here they were, blasted apart. One of them alone tonight. The other, tomorrow.

In the bedroom he heard the radio still playing; Elsbeth wasn't coming out—it shouldn't be taking her that long to turn off a radio and get her coat. He called, but she didn't answer. He didn't want to go up the hall—he couldn't ever remember being in her bedroom before, but, still, it was getting late. What could be keeping her? He called again. But still no answer. Maybe she couldn't hear over the radio. Or maybe something was wrong. He'd feel like an intruder going there, to her bedroom, but, still, what if something had happened? After all, she was old.

When he went up the hall, her coat was on the bed, and she was in front of the window.

"It's Bing Crosby," she said, "Bing Crosby!"

"Who?"

"On the radio, Deke! Bing Crosby! Can you believe it? 'White Christmas.'"

"Elsbeth, it's just that … ."

"I saw him, you know."

"You saw Bing Crosby? I never knew that."

"Yes … yes. I saw Bing Crosby. It was before the war. Mother took me. Oh, I tell you, how he could sing. When I went to Bryn Mawr—it was the only thing that made me special. My sister, you know, your grandmother, well, she had the looks. Maybe that's why Mother took me to see Bing Crosby … so that I could have a great story to tell. So I could say I'd been the one to see the most famous crooner in America.

"Other girls, well, they had other things. Monica Palmer she always claimed she'd had luncheon with Randolph Scott … I don't know if I believe that. But Bing Crosby! I was the only one who had actually seen him. He was handsome, you know. He doesn't get enough credit for that. But he was."

On an oriental carpet, her feet were tracing a dance. Deke recognized the fox trot—for Betsy and Whit's wedding he'd taken dancing lessons. He stepped into Elsbeth's pattern and, with every step, her white slip flashed out. And through her dress, he felt her bones, nearing the surface now, freeing themselves from the weight of flesh. Later, he'd hold an umbrella of hearts over her, and the footprints they made in the snow when they left his car would almost be gone by the time they sat down in the restaurant where she'd tell her blue velvet story. And maybe, this year, the one about Bing Crosby. And Whit and Betsy's kids would listen politely. Because that is what they'd been trained to do. And because they sensed in their great-great-aunt's words some distillation of their own history.

But, here, in this moment, over this carpet, knotted and cut by someone's long-ago fingers, his feet traced a pattern danced to a song sung by a man who'd been dead for decades. A man whose voice came from a box in a bedroom where Deke had never been before. A bedroom where a woman he'd known all his life slept every night. A woman who still had stories to tell.

So Deke held her. And he danced.

BANG!

———◆———

What it comes down to, Doc, is—Bang!—I lost my mind! Presto! Reducto! Had it. Lost it. Gone! *Alles kaput!* I don't really see what the big deal is. You know, whoever that asshole was who said a mind is a terrible thing to lose, Doc, had it all wrong. I mean look at me, for cryin' out loud. Three squares a day. Baskets of apples and stuff all over the place. Painting classes and crap. Not to mention the time I get to spend with a hottie like you. Can you believe it, Doc? No, sir, a mind most definitely is not a terrible thing to lose. I should know. I had one. Then bang! Oh, excuuuuuse me, Doc. Poor choice of words under the circumstances. What can I say? No pun intended, unless Freud was right … there really are no accidents. In which case, "bang" certainly was intended, but only by my subconscious. But as far as my mind goes, what can I say? Easy come, easy go. *Quod cito acquiritur cito perit.* Or whatever. People lose things all the time, Doc. I mean … their direction, their virginity, even their looks.

Think about that one, Doc. Kind of scary isn't it? I mean how is a hottie like you going to keep them down on the farm once old *tempus fugits. Kaput!* Botox can't redux.

Know what I think is interesting to lose? Your temper. Think about it, Doc. I mean, I have a temper. My brother's got a temper. You have a temper. All God's children got tempers.

But, how do we know we got them? Only by losing them, that's how. Your temper's there, but nobody can see it, or touch it, or hear it. It's just there, perking away. Then bang! You lose it. And suddenly everybody knows you've got one. Only you don't. Why? Because you've lost it. Weird, isn't it? I love metaphysical shit like this, don't you, Doc? It's so freaky.

Now, my dad. He's so temperless. Most of time he has absolutely no temper. He can't ... it's impossible, the way he's losing it all the time. He's a real Temperless Joe, my dad. I mean he loses his temper all over the place. The one person who can really find it is my mom. I mean she can find my dad's temper like that ... especially before they split. Now, not so much. But he loses his temper in other places too. Once, even in Headmaster Tilley's office. That was something to see ... the way he was screaming, I thought he was going to bust a gut. That was the time I threw a desk out the window. I mean, who knew? I mean throwing a desk seemed perfectly reasonable at the time. Shit. I thought I'd get the freshman Latin prize, you know? But that dickhead Gorman got it. I mean I lost out because that asshole Mr. Turner didn't like me. So I threw the desk. It seemed like a reasonable alternative to smacking Asshole Turner in his fat face. I still don't know what the big deal was. Of course, I should have been more careful. How was I supposed to know that Mrs. Tilley had picked that very moment to show the gardener where she wanted some flowers? Boy! Did my dad ever lose his temper when Headmaster Tilley told him I was suspended. And when we got home, too. That's when he really lost it. It was amazing. He must have found his temper somewhere in the car after we left school because he sure had it by the time we got home. He sure did.

But he's a good guy, you know, my dad. He really is. We can't complain, my sister Emily and my brother Peter and me. Some dads, when there's a divorce, they're such dicks. But our dad, he's okay… you know? He gets us almost every week-end. I can tell his girlfriend doesn't like it, but he still gets us. And after the shooting? He was the one who came. Have I told you that, Doc? I mean usually it's my mom who comes if there's something with Peter or me. But after the shooting, it was my dad. That's how I knew something had happened to Peter and that my mom had to be with him.

That dumb shit, Billingsley. Man. It was freaky, Doc. I got to tell you. Cops everywhere. And none of them had a clue. They were just letting their big fat cop guts spill over their belts like blubber awnings to keep their feet dry. See, they wanted to put us in the field house. After Columbine and all those other places, they knew they had to keep us together, so they wanted to put us in the field house, but it was being renovated. So they put us on the bleachers by the football field. And it started raining.

Man, it was weird … parents running up and down the rows of bleachers looking for their kids. Kids crying. And I don't just mean little kids, either. The faculty … man, they were freaky too. Some were saying Billingsley went into the faculty lounge and just shot the place up and a lot of them were dead. Nobody was saying how many kids had been shot. I kept look-ing for Peter, but they kept telling me to go back to the bleach-ers. Man, I didn't want to get suspended again, you know, Doc. I mean some colleges will overlook one suspension. But not two. So, I went back.

Everybody was surprised it was that asshole Billingsley. He was real quiet, you know. Not freaky. He was just real quiet. He never really hung out with anyone. He was freaky one way, though: his mother drove him to school every day. I mean, here he was a senior and his mother drove him to school. And, what gets me, is that he just lived a few blocks away. I mean that was weird, when you think about it.

People said it was because he didn't get accepted anywhere. And, man, that would do it to you. Twelve years at Pelham and not getting in anywhere. Man, that would do it. I
mean, that's what Pelham's all about, isn't it?—getting in
somewhere good. Did I tell you, my dad was third in his class?
And my uncle Deke, he was somewhere the hell up there, too.
Now I'm in this place, wondering if I'll be able to get into Hip
Hop Community College. All because of that dumb shit
Billingsley. Christ. Not to get in anywhere. Can you imagine
that? Not anywhere? No wonder he shot himself. I would, too.
Wouldn't you, Doc?

In a way, I was lucky. It started to rain, but I had my soccer
uniform on so at least my mom wouldn't freak about me getting my good pants wet. I kept standing up and looking down
the bleachers for Peter. I thought he'd spot me in my uniform.
I thought it would be easier for him to notice me. Peter, he's
such a little kid. And he does such weird stuff. He sleeps on
the floor. Did I tell you that, Doc? It freaks my mother out ...
he makes these nests on the floor with his blankets and sleeps
there. I call him birdbrain and he's so little and dumb he
doesn't even know I'm making fun of him. It's pathetic. So, I
wasn't too worried because, like I said, Doc, he does some
weird things, he could have been anywhere. But still, I wanted
to see him.

And then, Mrs. Tilley, she came and sat with me. She just
came and sat with me and put a blanket over me. After what I
almost did to her, I felt sort of bad about that, but I let her do
it. And she held an umbrella over me. It was getting dark, and
every time I could see headlights swinging into the drive, I
thought to myself, "That's Mom." Because, see, I still thought
it would be her that would come for us. But then, the way Mrs.
Tilley was holding the umbrella, I couldn't see the headlights
any more. I kind of pulled the blanket around my head and

just waited for whatever would come. And when I looked out again the bleachers were empty just about. There were a few kids from the middle school. But in the whole upper school, I was the only one left. And then I knew why Mrs. Tilley was being so nice to me. And then I saw my dad coming down the path ... I could just barely make him out, but it was him. And he had Uncle Deke with him. I stood up so they could see me. I just stood there and waited, you know? And my dad, he took the bleachers two at a time. He could do that because his legs are real long, Doc, you know? I'll probably be real tall, too, someday. But sometimes I hope not.

Sometimes, I just want to be real small. Like when I was under Mrs. Tilley's blanket. I kept having this crazy thought ... that I could become real small if I didn't move or anything ... you know, Doc? Like if I could just be perfectly still, that my organs and all my cells would just begin to move toward the center of my body . . what do they call it? . . . the soma? ... like it was a black hole or something. And that sooner or later I'd be so small no one could see me. Like I was a piece of dust or something.

But I'd be dense, you know, Doc. Really, really dense. So that if someone stepped on me, they'd feel me and say, "What the hell was that?" And I'd think to myself, "You dumb shit, you're so dumb you can't even see what's right under your foot. And even if you did, you'd just think I'm a piece of dust or something. But I'm right here." And I'd just sit there, not moving or anything, getting denser and denser and I be watching every move they made.

Isn't that metaphysical or what, Doc? Don't you just love metaphysical crap like that?

OTHER MEN'S SONS

———— ◆ ————

The April rain had cleared as quickly as it had come, and damp air surged over the check-out counter every time a Pelham Academy boy pushed through the supermarket doors. The boys, ruddy and broad-shouldered, joked up and down the deli counter and waited for corned beef sandwiches made for them by men in green aprons over blue shirts. Even the kid behind the register wore a tie.

"Will that be all, sir?" he asked Paul.

Stopping at the grocery had been a spur-of-the-moment impulse. When Jeremy, his son, had called earlier that day, Paul stunned everyone at the monthly managers meeting. He had to go, he said, he was sorry, he had to leave. Reese, his assistant, could carry on. He had only meant to buy a birthday present for Jeremy, the child of his first marriage, to give to the child of his second marriage, and then get on to St. Bart's Way where Jeremy was waiting. But there had been the rain, and he'd had to park a block away from the little gift shop. Suddenly, picking up some food seemed like a good idea.

But now everything he'd chosen seemed random: a bag of popcorn, some oranges, a carton of milk, none of it complementing anything else. Before his divorce, he had stopped at the store a couple of times a week, even had an arrangement with the weekend manager—slipping him a fifty every now and then to save a *Times* for after golf, but now nothing seemed to go together.

The wall by the last check-out was lined with every possible distillation of liquor. He remembered Penny, his first wife, once asking him to get ginger ale—Jeremy was sick, again— and coming home, saying, "There's nothing in that place that doesn't go with booze, for chrissakes." And he remembered, too, Jeremy coughing, forgetting to cover his mouth.

"Will there be anything else, sir?"

Paul grabbed a box of chocolate-crowned cookies. Two women were in line behind him. The older with a cake; the other, long-boned like Penny, holding a deli tray. Suppose, Paul thought, both women were to go to the house on St. Bart's Way. Suppose they were to offer their condolences with their cake and tray, saying, "I'm so sorry about Penny. Tell Jeremy, I'm so sorry about his mother. Tell Jeremy... " He could imagine himself watching them go down the brick walk, hearing them whisper, "That's him, isn't it? The ex-husband? How long had they been divorced?"

Four months earlier, Paul had been watching a fresh-faced Wharton grad on the trading floor when Jeremy called.

"Mom's sick."

Paul had said nothing. The Wharton grad had just made two hundred thousand dollars in two minutes and here was his own son, at nineteen, calling him at work, like a preschooler panicked over his mother being sick.

"Dad, did you hear me?"

"You said your mother's sick."

"Very sick."

"Has she seen a doctor?" What the hell was he supposed to do? He had been remarried for four years by then; he and Mia had a little girl named Madison.

"She's been seeing doctors for two weeks. She's had all the tests. She doesn't want chemo."

In the end, it had been that simple. And now here he was, trying to make sense of popcorn and milk. For a second, the signs over the deli counter, the bottles of liquor, even the check-out kid seemed freed from gravity's pull. Paul had to close his eyes and will them down.

When the kid at the check-out asked if he wanted paper or plastic, he could only say, "Yes."

Under the awning of the drug store where he used to buy Jeremy's Ritalin, Paul fished out his phone. The last of the Pelham boys were swinging their lacrosse sticks down the hill, the oldest of them now younger than his own son. Such easy confidence. He saw it radiating from the dewy young necks on the trading floor bent at their Bloombergs—knew too, Jeremy's chances for such self-assurance were growing dimmer every day.

Paul shifted the groceries and checked his watch, Mia's honeymoon gift, showing the times in London, New York, Tokyo. When he had called earlier, Mia had taken her mother and Madison out shopping—her parents were up from Norfolk for Madison's second birthday. Only her father, Donaldson, had been at the house, watching the early rounds of the Masters. How awkward that had been—telling his current father-in-law that his former wife had died.

Under the awning he got ahold of Mia; her voice sounded tight: "Paul, where are you? I called the office."

"The office? Why?"

"I didn't know where you were. Dad left a note. He said he was going over to the house on St. Bart's Way. I figured what must have happened. I'm—well, I'm sorry. Tell Jeremy, too, I'm sorry. Let me know what I can do."

"Why's your father over there?"

"I don't know. You know how he is." Her father Donaldson was such a wily old coot. A former submarine commander, Paul could never get a handle on him. Whenever they played golf, it was only nine holes; they'd have to invent stories of the back nine to tell their wives—the old boy's heart couldn't take any more. Paul suspected his father-in-law had made an art out of such deception. Once he'd slammed down his drink on the club house table, saying to Paul, "You know, I have trespassed. Mostly in fields of sweet voluptas, but God damn if anyone says I have sinned." Then he'd eyed Paul, daring him to comment.

"I'm going over there as soon as I get Jeremy something to give Madison for her birthday. He asked me to. He said he had promised Penny."

"Would you believe they spelled her name wrong?"

"Whose?"

"Maddy's. On the cake. They spelled her name wrong. I told them specifically two D's, but they still got it wrong."

"I have to get going. Everything's taking so long. He wanted me to get a jacket. I had to get a half dozen for him."

"You bought Jeremy a half dozen jackets?"

"He didn't know his size. The tailor gave me a half dozen. He said to let him pick the one he wants and bring the rest back."

"How could Jeremy not know his size?"

"I don't know. He just didn't. I have to go."

"I wasn't going to pay for it."

"For what?"

"The cake. But I thought, why not just ask for half off? So I did. Let me know if there's anything I can do. And don't let Dad eat anything he shouldn't."

The rain had started again, and Paul saw the two women duck their heads as they came out of the grocery. Damn their cakes and trays, the onset of their implacable rituals.

◆ ◆ ◆

The gift shop was a cathedral to civility. In that neighborhood, no homecoming, holiday or weekend visit went unobserved. How many Christmases, Mother's Days, and birthdays had he taken Jeremy there, saying "Watch where you're turning, Jeremy. Do you think Mommy'd like that? A mirror with a flower frame like that? Really? Don't you think she'd like this T-shirt with 'Jog to Beat the Jiggle'? You know how she likes to run." Paul picked out a plush elephant—it had lonely eyes.

He threw the elephant on top of the sport coats in their plastic bags on his back seat and checked his watch again— everything was taking so long—three hours since Jeremy had called. He pressed his speed dial.

"Dad, hey."

"Jeremy, listen, I'm sorry. I'm sorry … it's the rain and all. I'm on my way."

"It's OK. Donaldson is here."

"What?"

"Donaldson, you know, my step-grandfather. Or maybe I should say my virtual grandfather. Yeah, that's it … my virtual grandfather. He's here. Or I should say here and gone. Not really gone. Just for pizza."

"Pizza?"

"Yeah, neighbors, people keep bringing stuff. Cakes and stuff. I'm making a list so I can write Thank yous. I know you're supposed to do that. But I don't know. Frankly, some of this food turns my stomach. So Donaldson's gone for pizza. Double everything."

"I got the jackets. They let me take a half dozen."

"The present for Madison? Did you get that?"

"An elephant. I got her an elephant."

"That's cool. I mean an elephant is sure to be politically correct. Not really indigenous to one continent. Although, with Asian elephants, who knows how long before they're extinct, and then, how politically correct will elephants be?"

Where was it coming from, this manic cadence? These strange synaptic leaps?

"You sound a little tired, Jeremy."

"Well, maybe I'll sleep soon. I slept yesterday some. I don't know... You know what I think, Dad? I think political correctness is like courtly love, an unattainable ideal."

This disarming irony... so suggestive of a dormant intelligence. It had inspired so many parental false hopes.

"I got to go, Dad. Oxygen guy is here."

"Who?"

"Claude. The oxygen guy."

A surgeon's daughter, Penny had stepped onto St. Bart's Way like a homecoming queen, never noticing Paul watch his neighbors compute: "Maggio ... Maggio ... Italian." Since they knew he was Italian, he felt they knew the rest of his history: his father slouched in a chair, the old man's long fingers dangling over a cold can on the floor, never even looking up from the television when Paul told him he'd gotten into Georgetown.

First, the neighbors had offered, "Looks like rain, Paul," when he was putting out the trash, and then "Good to see you, Paul," as success came—many on St. Bart's Way had portfolios. And, finally, invitations for drinks on flagstone patios.

But then, there was Jeremy. At first, the boy had played with the neighbors' sons. "Like little fishes," Penny had said, watching them from the sunroom. "They flow across the lawns like a school of fish." But then the others swam ahead, sensing the ocean beyond, readying themselves for it, and Jeremy had stayed behind, entangled in the tentacles of vague disorders … dyslexia, ADD, ADHD …

And then there was the divorce, and Paul returning to St. Bart's Way and seeing Jeremy peering out the side panes beside the door. And Penny refusing to come from the kitchen.

Now, on the front porch where he'd once hung the Christmas wreath around the eagle knocker, Paul felt like an interloper again. In the driveway was a white panel truck with "Home Health Services" on its side. No sign of Donaldson's black Lincoln. Paul shifted the sports coats in their plastic bags to the arm carrying the elephant and opened the door.

Jeremy was kneeling before two oxygen tanks, and coils of plastic tubing laced through the living room to the sunroom where a man was disassembling a hospital bed. When the boy flicked his hair back, Paul saw the exhaustion ringing his eyes.

"Dad, hey, I didn't hear you."

"Well, I just let myself in."

"Donaldson's here. He's gone for pizza. We got to disassemble this stuff, or else they'll charge us for another day. Oxygen-guy Claude is here."

"So I see." Everything about the boy seemed exaggerated and oddly detached. When he introduced Claude, he was overeager, almost giddy. Paul watched the health service man's eyes telegraphing, So, you finally got here, you son of a bitch.

"What can I do to help?" Paul asked.

"Oh, I guess, we've got things pretty well under control," Claude said. He picked up two pieces of the bed and went to the truck. Jeremy picked up another piece and what looked like an inflatable mattress. Paul stood alone in the living room with the oxygen tanks with their gauges. Had Jeremy been the one checking them? Monitoring them? Had Penny, in her most desperate time, trusted him, their dreamy son, with the last complexities of life? And had she done it so the boy could realize his own strengths?

Paul went into the sunroom and watched his son and Claude loading the truck. The big man slammed the door and hugged Jeremy to him, rocking him from side to side. Paul saw the boy's shoulders convulse. Then stop. Then the boy ducked away, his hair hanging over his eyes, and the truck backed into the street and drove away.

"Donaldson should be here soon," Jeremy said when he came in the front door.

"I got your sport coats and the present for Maddy," Paul said. Jeremy reached in the bag with the elephant, tearing it some, and pulled out the plush toy. He stroked it as if to coax some comfort from it, and Paul felt embarrassed for the childishness of his son's caresses. But said nothing.

"Mom wanted me to be sure to give Madison something. I don't know why. I guess I could have given her one of those." A parade of bears strutted across the sunroom radiator. "People send such stupid stuff."

"You look a little tired, Jeremy."

"I'll catch up later."

"Why don't you try to lie down?"

"No!"

"Okay. It's just that … ."

"I'm not ready to sleep. I'll sleep when I'm ready." The boy tried on a sport coat. He was all bone and flashing elbows. Like Dad, Paul thought. He remembered his own mother, ramrod straight in the haberdashery, buying a suit for the old man, the second he would ever own, and that the one he would be buried in, and her saying, "Forty-four, long. He's a forty-four long." Even before the boy's arm was through the sleeve, Paul could see the coat was too small.

"This looks great, don't you think, Dad?" he said.

"Like it was made for you, Jer."

"I should have called you, Dad."

"You did, Jer." The boy had phoned regularly at first. Then more frequently, but more erratically—once when Paul and Mia were making love. Another time at four thirty in the morning. Then, suddenly, the calls stopped. Just stopped.

"I should have done what she wanted," the boy said. His hair was hanging over his forehead; Paul couldn't see his eyes.

Donaldson's Lincoln slid to the curb. They watched the old man in his yellow golfing sweater put the pizzas on the car's roof. "I better go help him," said Paul.

"I'll go." The boy thrust the elephant back in the bag, tearing it more.

The sunroom was empty except for a chair, the bears, and a pot with a plastic angel stuck next to a sagging plant. Paul watched the old man and his son get the food, the spit-and-polish naval officer and his son with the cuffs of his jeans soaking up the damp like denim wicks. Jeremy laughed at something Donaldson said as the big man took a bulging paper bag from the backseat. Paul couldn't make out their words, but he wanted to be part of it.

"They'll kill you with their casseroles," Donaldson was saying when they came in. "It's a fact. A friend of mine ... his wife died. So many neighbor ladies fed him so many damn casseroles, he was dead in six months. It's a fact."

When he said "Hey, Paul," Paul felt diminished. Why had the old man come? What did he want? Paul tried to think if he had even ever met Penny. What was he doing here?

The boy took the bag from Donaldson, and Paul saw the old man's brow glistening—his heart?

"Watch the bag," Donaldson said. "It's got subs in it. And keep your hands off the liverwurst. My heart can't take pizza. Burns like hell. The docs say stay away from red meat. But what the hell? They never said anything about gray meat. So I eat all the liverwurst I can lay my hands on. Man, that with a few onions ... ."

Carrying the jackets up the stairs, Paul tripped on one of the plastic bags, and the elephant rolled down a few steps. Donaldson caught it, carried it up the stairs, using the banister to hoist his weight.

In Jeremy's room, the old man said, "Hell of a thing, this." Paul thought he meant the room: every surface—the desk, the bookcase, the bureau—all heaped with clothes, CDs, magazines, books. Skis slouched in a corner. And speakers, big as chairs, small as robins' nests. One camera lay on the desk. Another dangled from the headboard. The sheet on the bed, the color of old snow.

But the old man hadn't meant the mess.

"How old was she?" he asked Paul.

The arithmetic of their ages had been one of their omens when he met Penny in the Georgetown library: three years, three months, three days difference between them.

"Fated," they had laughed when they became engaged.

"Forty-five," Paul said to Donaldson. "She was forty-five."

But what was that to the old man? Paul watched him taking it all in, the skimpy sheet, the heap of tennis shoes, but there was no judgment in his eyes, only the search for some bittersweet familiar. The old man grunted and scooped up something from behind the lamp; it rattled. When he opened his fist, Paul saw a vial of sleeping pills with Penny's name on it. The old man slipped it into his sweater.

✦ ✦ ✦

They sat on the patio and Paul looked out over the lawn slipping into black and remembered another damp evening, remembered trying to mow the lawn and a five-year-old saying,

"Let me push, Daddy. Let me push." Jeremy wedging himself in front of Paul so that Paul had to arch his back and could barely control the machine. And Penny at the door in her running shorts—God, such legs—and smiling and not realizing that arching his back was killing Paul, and Jeremy insisting, "Let me do it alone, Let me do it alone, Daddy," and trying to push Paul's hands from the handle, and suddenly, hitting a bump and the handle snapping up, under the boy's chin, splitting it, and Penny glaring at Paul all the way to the emergency room. And all the way home.

And now the boy sat across from him, the cuff of his sport coat dipping into the pizza, and Paul saying nothing. He watched his boy relax into the downy comfort of his third beer, his lips pursing toward the can as tenderly as if it were a woman's mouth. Paul saw Donaldson register the boy's ravening, then take the vial from his pocket and dump half the pills into his own beer.

"Ever wonder what whales drink?" the old man asked.

"What?" the boy's interest was piqued, but his eyes refused to acknowledge the pills or how he intended to use them.

"Ever wonder what whales drink? Think about it. With all that water and not a drop of it fresh, what do they drink? They're mammals like we are, after all."

Paul, knowing to stay out of it, watched the boy smile, still refusing embarrassment for the vial: "Okay, what do whales drink?"

"Beer."

"You're telling me whales drink beer?"

"We'd surface, see. The sub. And there'd be a whale. Well, subs, you know, they're so cramped sometimes you do anything to relieve tension. They had this game to see who could hit a whale with a beer. The one nearest the blow hole won. Of course the beer had to be open, otherwise it wouldn't do the whale any good." The old man arced his beer toward a dog-wood, iridescent with blooms. Paul saw the challenge in the old man's eyes as he turned toward Jeremy. Saw the old man's eyes travel from the half-full vial to the beer cupped in the boy's fist. The boy dumped the pills into the beer and tossed it toward the blooming tree.

Paul watched the old man gentle his son away from his craving. No embarrassment. No humiliation. He, who had led other men's sons through the maze of the market, sat and watched a man he knew only through happenstance distract his own son from surpassing sorrow. The game got raucous: Donaldson using a rusty poker from the grill as a golf club; Jeremy, a long-handled barbecue fork as a bat. The cans pinging in the twilight, rousing a neighbor's dog, and Paul looking around for something of his own to whack away with. But he couldn't find anything. He considered getting a long-handled spoon, but getting something from the house, well, that would look desperate. Still, they kept playing, cheering their hits, goading each other, until, still empty-handed, Paul saw sweat on Donaldson's lip.

"Better get those cans up before the neighbors complain. The dogs are all stirred up," Paul said.

His remark interrupted the boy mid-swing. "You know, she wanted me to call you, Dad."

"You did, Jer. You called."

"No. She wanted you to come over."

"Over here?"

"Yeah. At the end. I think she wanted you to come over. At least I think that's what she said."

"You're not certain?"

"They gave her a lot of medicine, you know, Dad."

"Why didn't you call?"

"What if I had? What the hell would that have proved?"

The boy brushed past and, before he went into the kitchen, threw his fork at the dogwood. Paul stayed outside. From the patio he could see his son through the window, rooting around in the refrigerator. Paul looked at Donaldson, but the old man was picking up beer cans.

When Paul went into the kitchen, the boy was digging into the back of the refrigerator, bottles of soda were toppling over, rolling onto the floor. An orange fell out and went under the table.

Jeremy's head was nearly knocking into the light above the top shelf. He was shoving aside casseroles and cartons of milk.

"Jer," Paul asked, "what are you doing?"

"Looking, okay? I'm looking for something, okay? I can't sleep." He took his head out of the refrigerator. Paul could see that the tag on the sport coat where it had dipped into the pizza was dripping red, but he didn't say anything.

"Jer … ."

"I can't sleep."

"Why didn't you call, Jer?"

"What would that have proved? That you are some great hero? Coming at the last minute?" The boy's face, his whole lanky body, was contorting. "All it would have proved was that you're a prize-assed dick. Like I really need any proof of that. I mean, why didn't you come that time the car got smashed up? Or when the plumbing went and we had to go shit at the neighbors' for three days? Why didn't you come then? You big, come-at-the-last-minute kind of superhero. I didn't call you because I didn't want to. I just didn't want to."

The boy was collapsing against the refrigerator door, but it kept swinging and couldn't support him. The boy's rage, Paul knew, was grief-driven and maybe even what he himself deserved, but still he wanted to hit him, if only to make him stop.

He took a step toward him, but the boy sobbed: "They took all the morphine. And I can't sleep. I had to keep myself awake for so long … I was afraid I wouldn't hear her. I kept thinking when she was gone the morphine would be mine, but the hospice people took it all. I didn't know they'd do that. I kept thinking that it would help me. But they dumped it out."

Paul went to him and tried to hold him, cursing that he didn't have his father's height, that all he had to offer his son was his own, shorter shoulder.

"It's okay, Jer."

"She wanted me to tell you to come. But I never called, so that's how she went, thinking you didn't come on purpose. I'll never forgive myself for that. Christ, I'll never forgive myself. What am I going to do? I can't sleep." Paul patted and patted the jacket still stiff against his son's bones.

Neither of them had seen the old man come in. He filled the doorway. "Who do you think you are—God?"

Paul and his son stared at the old man.

"Well, you're not God, Goddamn it," Donaldson said. You can't forgive yourself. Nobody can do that … forgive themselves. That's for God. He's the one who says if we're forgiven or not."

The old man's sweater was garish under the kitchen's florescence.

"Maybe we can forgive each other. I don't know. But forgive ourselves? That's for God. What the hell … we all do things. But we all do the best we can, too. That's all any of us can… the best we can. We're only human. It's in the Bible forgive us our sins—that belongs to God."

The boy, still within Paul's arms, grounded himself in humor: "Yeah, and a few minutes ago you were the one telling me whales drink beer."

The old man, too, retreated to joking: "You doubt my word, boy?"

And they volleyed put-downs back and forth until Jeremy went to take a shower.

✦ ✦ ✦

Paul looked away as Donaldson slapped his palm on his Lincoln's roof for leverage and lowered himself into it. "God, what a helluva thing," the old man said, nodding toward the house. "And for you, too. You were her husband, once, for Chrissake. Still, for you, people will know. What'll they think? Hell, who knows? Not being able to tell anyone. Now, that was a helluva thing. You know how it goes."

So that was why the old man had come—to warm himself in the afterglow of a secret woman. Paul knew at that moment, whoever she had been, the sheer joy and celebration of her was as alive to the old man as if the woman herself were walking down St. Bart's Way, the streetlights catching her one by one.

"It's so damned hard, you know, life is," the old man went on, struggling with his seatbelt. "Still, you got to ask yourself, what are we given life for if not to live it?" He got the buckle into the slot and closed the door. Paul watched him drive away.

Jeremy was still in the shower when he went back into the house: Paul wanted to tell him he would spend the night. When the boy stood before him, Paul saw it was worse than he had imagined. Not only the boy's ribs, but his hips, too, protested against his flesh. Paul couldn't let the boy think that he had failed his mother, couldn't let him think that because he hadn't called, he deserved every bad thing that would come his way.

He offered this, "Maybe ... "

"What, Dad?"

"Maybe I had it coming. If I had stayed, you wouldn't have

had reason to break your word. I guess that's mine to live with."

"What do you say, Dad, that we don't get into this right now? Whether your great swinging mea culpa is bigger than my great swinging mea culpa. Okay?"

When Paul went to check later, the boy was already asleep, the only ordered thing in the room, the sport coat draped over a chair. Paul tried to close the window over the desk—the April air was too raw for the boy's wet hair—but he couldn't get proper leverage—the heap on the desk would crash to the floor. He wished again for his father's height, but the window was stuck, and his son's hair had to be cold, and chill would corrode the comfort the boy had earned.

It had been, what—seven, eight years since he'd gone into the bedroom in the front of the house? The rug, the wallpaper, all the same. Only the bed was different. Pushed to the window overlooking the street. Had this been Penny's last entertainment before the sunroom? Watching neighbors? The children to school? The cleaning women? The mailman? And had the boy been beside her, offering his humor, and Penny letting him know she trusted him, her dreamy son, with her final hours?

Ever since Jeremy called that morning, Paul had had some sense of her close by, some private, forgiving sense of her understanding that he'd never have wanted this ending. That even with all the fighting and bitterness, he had never wanted for there not to be a Penny.

Paul went to the closet where she stored the blankets. There, on the floor, lonely as puppies, were her running shoes —those legs. Still, what had they been against the afternoon he first saw Mia's delicate fingers dancing on the Bloomberg?— Paul not taking the mouse from her small hand with its pink nails, but covering her hand with his, and saying, "I only want the yen," although he knew perfectly well where the yen was, and Mia, not looking away from the screen, breathing in his ear, "Is it only the yen you want, Mr. Maggio? Or is it the desire?" And so the race had been won.

Paul picked up one of the shoes and put his hand in, feeling the imprint of toes on a sole he couldn't see, then he took a blanket and went down the hall. When he spread it over Jeremy, he saw his son's breathing relax. So, too, did the lids of his eyes, as though no longer fearing the sleep he needed would seep through them and leak into the wakened world.

NEAR SUNSET

———◆———

Tie already stripped off and white cuffs folded back, Harry Sodermain holds their everyday tumblers under the ice-maker. "So when did he call?"

Martha's chopping carrots on the kitchen island, the jute lanyard from her glasses swinging like a loose jib line. Below the hem of her khaki skirt, blue veins lace her ankles, and her moccasins squeak on the glossy, dark floor.

"About ten. I was just on my way to take Coco to the vet's." She turns to a recipe propped on a clear, plastic stand. "I know I'm forgetting something ... something. Oh well."

Harry watches her running a finger up and down the recipe, then carries their tumblers to an array of amber liquor near the French doors. Behind the bottles, a window overlooks a sweep of back yard that, even in October, holds the vivid green of a springtime pasture. Between his neighbors' houses and tall trees, the sunset blazes pink and orange above a low, purple ribbon.

"So he called at ten?" Harry splashes more bourbon into one tumbler than the other.

"Yes, about ten," Martha says. "I already had Coco's leash on. She thought we were going for a walk. To see her leaping around, you'd never know she had to go to the vet's. When Peter called, she was barking so much I had to lock her in the mudroom. Let's see, I put in the shrimp, the orzo. Oh, well." Scooping the carrots against her knife, she plops them into a blue enamel casserole.

"So what did he say?" Harry carries the tumblers back to the refrigerator where poodle magnets hold a flurry of fall notices: a lecture titled *Scott and Zelda in Baltimore, the Sad Sojourn* at the Historical Society, a noontime discussion on *The Shepherdless among Us* at St. David's. This last is circled in red.

"Only that his area code has changed. Apparently the one in Miami is too full, so his neighborhood got a new one. I wrote it down." Martha puts the casserole into the oven and sets the timer. The red seconds and minutes begin counting down.

"So his own number didn't change again?"

"No. Just his area code is different... he wanted us to know. Those carrots have to cook. What with Peter's calling and all, I was too late for Dr. Steinwald to see Coco. I had to leave her with someone new, a Dr. Wu."

"Did you tell this new guy she's passing blood?"

"He wants to do some tests. He'll call us tomorrow. Do you want something? That orzo will take a while."

"We're nearly out of bitters."

"Write that down for me, so I don't forget." Martha washes the knife.

On a blackboard wreathed with scraps of paper pinned to its frame, Harry writes "bitters," and starts rooting around in a French country hutch with shelves full of bright soup tureens and photographs in silver frames. The pictures are mostly of himself and Martha and their three children. In the largest, they are all on a dock: Eric in his Dartmouth sweatshirt, Polly with her big smile, and Peter with his lamb-like eyes staring past the camera toward something the others aren't interested in.

"What are you looking for?" Martha hangs the knife blade on a magnetized strip.

Harry is still looking in the hutch. "I want some chalk. There's just a nub left on that string by the blackboard."

"The stores still have some back-to-school supplies. They're getting their Christmas stuff, but they should have some chalk left. I'll get it, but write it by the bitters. If it's not written down, it's like it doesn't exist for me these days."

Harry tries to close the drawer, but it sticks and when he shoves it a picture topples over, the only one in black and white —Peter, older now. On the cusp of manhood. On the deck of a sailboat, in jeans and a sunburst T-shirt. The angle of the light says the picture was taken near sunset. Harry rubs his thumb up and down the silver frame, then sets the picture back in its place.

"Do you want some cheese?" Martha asks. "Or how about hummus?"

"Cheese would be good." Harry writes bitters and chalk with a white nub and carries both tumblers out the French doors to the patio where a thick vine of small roses covers a white trellis. Along the patio's edge, candles in globes with plastic webbing sit at even intervals, as if someone took four steps and set a candle down, took another four and set another down. Harry puts Martha's tumbler on the table and runs his thumb up and down his own, cutting a wide, wet ribbon in its frost. On St. Bart's Way everything is very quiet. When he pulls out his chair, its iron legs grate and clang on the flagstones.

The summer had been dry and hot, and the early October weather is still warm. At the end of his yard, the dogwood blazes to scarlet, but a few curled, dusky leaves, like wisps of newly sheered dark wool, litter the flagstones, Harry notices.

Martha carries out a basket of crackers and a red disk of

cheese with a few slices cut from it. "I forgot the knife," she says.

"This is enough," Harry says. "I don't need any more."

"I'll just be a minute. Don't wait for me," she says.

Harry doesn't drink until she comes back with a knife and takes a sip from her tumbler. Then he takes a deep swallow.

"What did he say?"

"Oh, we just talked about Coco. I told him it was still warm up here."

"So mainly he wanted us to know about his area code?"

"Yes. I wrote it down somewhere."

"So that was it?"

"He said he might be bringing a boat up from St. Augustine next month. A sixty-footer."

"So he's still doing that boat thing? What do they call them? Boat runners?"

"Yes. Boat runners."

"Helluva thing to call them."

"Well, that's what they're called. People want their boats one place or another and don't have time to do it themselves. He said he was up in Halifax this summer."

"Halifax?"

"Part of a four-man crew."

"You'd think he'd have more sense than to go anywhere near Canada."

"That was a while ago, Harry. He was just the cook. How could a cook have known what they were up to? He was only nineteen."

"Talk about tempting fate. Jeez … going to Canada again!"

"Well, he went. And nothing happened."

"Not that we know of."

"I should have brought out some napkins." Martha starts to get up.

148

"It's okay. Don't bother. This is fine." Harry puts some cheese on a cracker.

Martha sits down and twists her mouth. She looks out over the expanse of lawn, where the purple border has darkened and is pushing back the pink.

"I saw a flock of robins in that dogwood this morning," she says. "A whole flock. They were eating all the berries. You usually only see flocks in the spring. Hardly ever in the fall. I guess they were congregating so they could fly south."

"So he's bringing up a sixty-footer. Where to? Annapolis?"

"I don't know. I guess so. He said he expected to be in Maryland sometime next month."

"Why would anyone want their boat in Annapolis in November? Only fools race on the bay in the winter. Everyone knows the Chesapeake is hell in winter."

Martha puts down a cracker. "My gosh, the pesto! That's what I forgot ... the pesto! I had to make an extra stop just to get it." A shrill edge has crept into her voice. "I stopped deliberately to get it and there I go and forget it. My mind is such a sieve these days." When she pushes back her chair, her glasses swing from their lanyard and slap the tabletop.

She goes into the kitchen, and Harry puts down his drink and cups his fist over his mouth. He stares out over his back yard, where, through the open garage door, the angle of the setting sun enflames the rear reflector on a rusting bicycle fender.

Martha comes out. "Good thing I had to go in. The recipe calls for only a cup and a half of chicken broth, but it really needs more. The orzo still wasn't soft. It would have been like eating pebbles. I should make a note ... two cups."

"What else did he say? Anything?"

"I didn't want to tell him I had to get to the vet's; I didn't want to cut him off. But Coco was going crazy. She didn't know what was happening. She seemed more energetic today. Maybe that blood isn't anything. The Watsons' poodle lived to fourteen."

"How'd he sound?"

"Fine."

"He sounded okay?"

"He sounded fine, you know, like himself. I told him I was trying to get that new biography of Rilke. You remember, he wrote that paper on Rilke."

"I thought that was Erik. I thought Erik wrote on Rilke."

"It was Peter."

"You're probably right."

"I know I am. Twenty-five pages on Rilke—'the point of life is to fail at greater and greater things.' He got a B because it was late."

"Is he taking the inland waterway, or sailing up the coast?"

Martha draws a sudden intake of breath. "You know, I didn't think to ask. I should have thought to ask."

"The coast can be rough in November."

In the kitchen the phone rings and Martha starts to get up.

"Don't bother," Harry tells her. "It's probably someone from Calcutta calling about refinancing our mortgage."

Martha pushes back her chair. "It could be Dr. Wu. Maybe he's got the test results early. He said he'd call tomorrow, but maybe he's got them already."

Harry sits alone. Against the twilight's purple border, the dogwood has deepened to mahogany. The cicadas have started, and the cubes in Harry's tumbler clink. But everything else outside is still.

Inside, Martha's voice has taken on that rising intonation it always does when she's about to say goodbye. Harry waits, but she doesn't come out. He waits longer and hears nothing in the kitchen. No oven opening. No refrigerator door. No moccasins. Nothing. Through the French doors he can see past the liquor bottles to the mud room doorknob where Martha's pouch of a handbag hangs.

He drains his glass and goes in.

She's holding a battered brown address book with gaps like missing teeth where some of its alphabet tabs are gone. The "S" hangs by a prayer.

"Was that him on the phone?" Harry asks. "Was that Peter?"

"No, no, it was the vet's. Some little assistant or something." Martha's glasses slip from her nose and swing on their lanyard. She tries putting them back on, but they fall off again. She keeps flipping through the address book.

"What are you looking for?"

"That paper. I told you, I wrote Peter's new area code on a piece of paper. Somehow, when the vet's called, I just realized I didn't remember what I did with it." The kitchen timer bleeps and jerks her head like a slap. She puts down the address book and yanks open the oven door. She sends the casserole cover clattering onto the island, tastes the orzo, then punches more numbers into the timer.

"Why did the vet's call?" Harry says.

"What?" She puts the casserole back into the oven.

"Coco's tests ... why did the vet's call?"

"Some little assistant ... she wanted me to know that I'd left Coco's leash there. She said they didn't know whose it was, so they let all the dogs sniff it and when they held it under Coco's nose, she whined so they knew it was hers."

Her voice sounds shrill again. She goes back to the address book, turns it upside down and shakes it by its covers. The pages dangle like the body of a dead sea bird held by its wings, but nothing falls out. "I'm losing everything. I didn't remember to get the pesto when I got the orzo. I had to make an extra trip. Now the paper with Peter's number. I don't know what I did with it."

"Maybe you put it in your bag."

"What?"

"Your handbag. Maybe it's there." Harry goes around the island to the blackboard.

Martha leaves the address book and gets her handbag from the doorknob. "This thing has so many pockets. I bought it so I could keep things straight. But I can never remember what's in what pocket. I swear it eats things. I put things in, and they just disappear." She dumps her wallet and keys on the counter. With his knuckle, Harry skims the papers pinned around the blackboard, and they flutter after his touch. "You know, directory assistance will give you the new area code if you call the old one. It's all automated now. You just call the old one," he tells her.

Martha keeps rooting in her handbag. "I'll never find it. I'm losing everything." The kitchen timer bleeps again and she stares at it as if it were a midnight summons.

"We could do that," Harry says.

"Do what?"

"Call the old area code. They'll give you the new one."

"Oh." She jams her handbag onto the counter, and a lipstick rolls out. She hesitates between picking it up and going to the oven. She goes to the oven. Harry watches her but keeps his finger on the notices. His knuckle slowly circumnavigates the rim of the blackboard twice more before it stops.

"Is this it? Five-six-one?" He takes a little square of paper from the frame. "Is this it?" he says.

"What did you say?" Martha's moccasins squeak as she pivots from the oven to the island with the casserole.

"Is this it?" Harry says. "Five-six-one. That's all it says ... five-six-one."

Martha stands still. "I knew I put it somewhere. I remember writing it. I should put it in the book right now. If I wait until we eat, I'll forget." Martha takes the lid off the casserole and the scent of shrimp fills the kitchen like incense.

"You take care of that. I'll take care of his number," Harry says. Under "Peter Sodermain" are numbers for San Diego, Duluth, Provincetown, Vancouver, Galveston and Miami. And for the Pacific Haven Clinic. The Desert Springs Treatment Center. He writes the new area code by the Miami number and puts the book away. He picks up Martha's lipstick and then sets out two wineglasses.

"Red with that?" he says.

"Yes, there's shrimp in it, but I think red would be good." Martha's slicing a baguette she's taken from the bread drawer. "I bought a new kind of butter. It's from France. They whip it some way so it has half the calories. At least that's what it says."

"Leave it to the French to fill something with air and charge twice as much." Harry looks at her, but there's no smile. She checks to make certain the oven is off.

Harry puts down the corkscrew he's twisting. "Don't worry about Coco," he tells her. "She'll be okay."

"I'm not worried about Coco. That's what's wonderful about dogs. They don't know what's coming. They always think everything will be okay." Martha keeps slicing. Her glasses slip.

"You know, after we eat, maybe I should give Burt Greene a call," Harry says.

Martha puts the bread in a basket. "Why?"

"Well, Burt and I, we have lunch once in a while, and every fall, he gives me this song and dance about wanting to get his cabin cruiser down to the islands. Then, come February, it's the same thing from him, 'Geez, if I only had managed to get my boat down south, Harry.' Nobody sings the blues like Burt."

"So you think he might want Peter to take it down?"

"It's worth a shot. Peter'll be up here in November. He knows the waters. That way he can make money coming and going. And I was thinking … "

"What?" Martha holds the basket of bread.

Harry pours the wine. "Well, if Peter's up here for November, maybe he'll stick around until Thanksgiving."

"What about Burt Greene's boat?"

"I don't even know if Burt will want Peter to take it south, and if he does, what's another week or two? I've thrown some business his way over the years. If I ask him to wait a bit, he'll probably do it. He's a decent sort." Harry watches Martha check the oven again. She asks him if he wants to eat in or out.

"Out," he says. "Why not? Might as well do it while we can."

"So, you want to eat on the patio?"

"Yes, the patio. Who knows how many nice days we have left?"

He carries the wine outside. The sky's vivid colors are all gone, and the dogwood is a dark silhouette against an expanse of silver slipping to black. Harry sets the glasses on the table. From the patio's edge, he chooses a yellow candle and picks out the dried leaves caught in its webbing. To get the match near the wick, he has to tilt the globe. The flame sputters, then catches, blue in its center. When Harry sets the globe between the two glasses, the wine lights to burgundy. Everything is quiet. Harry sits down. And he waits.

STANDARDS

———————◆———————

Years later, whenever Elise Babcock thought about the Sunday afternoon Charlie Pierce came through her hedge, she would remember the sound of his voice. How its low timbre suggested that here was a steady man. So steady that when Charlie handed her his car keys, saying "Take it," she had reached with no more hesitation than if she were thrashing in twenty-foot waves and he'd tossed her a lifesaver.

The horrible afternoon Charlie came through her hedge, the Baltimore July sky was cataract-white, and she'd been trying to cope with the tumor in her husband's brain since February. And all the people who had said, "Call me if you need anything, Elise," were off to their beach houses.

That afternoon, Tommy's feet rested in a puddle of Sunday papers scattered on an old Heriz of his grandmother's, and their two older children were in the back yard near the garage. Molly holding her ratty doll and watching Stenson work at his bike with a screwdriver and wiping his sniffling nose.

Twenty minutes earlier Elise had smacked Stenson, her oldest, across his mouth. For the hundredth time, he had asked her about getting his bike fixed, and she had yelled not to bother her about it again—she was sick of hearing about his Goddamned bike. Full of a ten-year-old's rage, Stenson had screamed back, "You're so stupid. All you do is smoke. Even your farts smell stupid."

From the sunroom's French doors, Elise watched Molly start walking her doll's pink legs from spoke to spoke on the bike's rear wheel. "Oh Christ," Elise said and shifted their youngest, Oliver, on her hip to get a cigarette from her shorts.

"What?" Tommy was wearing thick socks and sandals and one of the good shirts he used to reserve for court dates. His "chemo hair" had grown back frizzled.

"Oh, it's Molly." Elise contorted herself around Oliver's bottom to light the match. "She just hovers around Stenson all the time. It pisses him off. I should have sent them both to camp. But you were in treatment when the applications were due." Months before she would have bit back a statement like that, but months before Tommy's cancer hadn't metastasized and withered whatever had been decent and brave in herself. That horrible afternoon, her remark's bitterness felt almost as good as a jolt of cold vodka going down to her gut.

Suddenly, Stenson grabbed the doll and threw it. Molly was running away before the doll landed, but Stenson ran after her. Blinded by a blood lust, the boy never saw the driveway's edge waiting to trip him.

"Oh, Christ." Elise turned to Tommy, but he didn't seem up to taking Oliver. "Oh, Christ!" And she was out the door.

Stenson was kneeling, blood streaming down his chin, his hand cupping it, red running through his fingers, his primal howl piercing the Sunday quiet. Oh, Christ. Oliver was on her hip and wailing in commiseration with his brother, and then screaming louder when she put him down to look under the flap sliced into Stenson's chin and see driveway grit. And Oliver was at her leg, screaming "Up. Up." And Stenson's blood was all over her hands. Oh, Christ. Christ. And then she was running past Tommy, useless, as he came across the lawn. And she was running for ice and yelling at Stenson, "Sit down. Sit down," because he could faint. And hit his head. And then what would she do?

And when she had the ice wrapped in a towel and was halfway back to all of them who claimed pieces of her, Charlie Pierce came through her hedge. A gray-haired paunch in a red polo shirt. But tall. Very tall.

He looked at Stenson's chin. "He's going to need stitches."

"I know." She held the towel under Stenson's jaw. "I just want to stop the bleeding a bit. Put your head back, Stenson. Put it back! I need my keys." But when she had them, Charlie and Tommy were looking at her car where it slouched on a tire rim, blocking Tommy's.

"Shit," Elise said. "Oh, Christ."

Oliver started clutching her leg. "Up. Up." Trying to get him, Tommy stumbled, and the toddler ran away, screaming.

"Can you drive a stick?" Charlie said.

"It's been a long time," Elise said.

"It'll come back to you. Take mine. Take it. I'll look after your little guy and your daughter. I have a woman who helps me with my wife. I'll call her."

And so Elise took Charlie Pierce's keys, his hand on her shoulder, steering her through the hedge and his voice telling her to take Stenson to Johns Hopkins.

"He just needs stitches, but that's where you need to take him. Trust me. Take him to Hopkins, not some suburban place. Someone will take the car."

And someone did. The waiting room was full, but someone took Stenson first. And someone brought him a stuffed bear to hold and then two more when he said he had a sister and a brother. And someone asked Elise if she wanted a cup of coffee. And the doctor gave her a vial of codeine pills "so she wouldn't have to stop on the way home." All these services moving in smooth syncopation, orchestrated by someone.

When Tommy first had told her who had bought the hulking house next door, she hadn't believed him. But he insisted. A senior partner at his law firm had gone to Yale with the old guy, he said. They definitely were *those* Pierces. The Pierces who once owned a California railroad and now a family of mutual funds. The Pierces whose money was molten magma floating under international markets.

"It's something about his wife. That's why they're here," Tommy had said. "She has some sort of mental condition. Apparently he's found a doctor who's doing her some good. You know Baltimore. People get a pair of shoes custom-made in London and then wear them for twenty-five years. They see nothing incongruous about having them resoled again and again, and dropping their Maestro's Circle check for the symphony on their way to the shoemaker's. Baltimore's the perfect place to hide. Nobody flaunts anything here."

When Elise got home, Tommy and Charlie were watching a ballgame in the sunroom, Oliver was asleep on the old oriental with his thumb in his mouth, and a rich, familiar aroma floated from the kitchen.

"I hope you don't mind," Charlie said. "I had Vannie, the woman I told you about, stop and get some things. I didn't think you'd feel like cooking."

"The kids will be glad. My culinary skills have been reduced to cold cereal." Elise handed Charlie his keys. "You saved my life."

Molly stepped into the doorway. "We're going to have chicken, Mom. Chicken!" Her ratty doll's wide eyes were nearly popping out of their skull.

Charlie got up from the couch. "Well, you folks are in for

a treat. Vannie's chicken is the best. I keep telling her she should open a little restaurant."

"Can't you stay?" Elise said, her tone inflected with neutral civility.

"No … no. Thanks, not tonight. I've got to get back. My wife doesn't like being alone too much." His words were carefully modulated, and the phrase weighted with just enough explanation to quash queries. It sounded as if he were giving a recitation. As if he knew that the listener, as if all listeners, knew about his wife, and long ago he had parsed out the phraseology to frame her condition exactly how he wanted it understood.

But at the French doors his voice rose. "Maybe you could come over for drinks. Both of you. About eight. I've asked Vannie to stay. It's been a long day. She can stay with the children."

Elise watched him walk back through her hedge. She was thirty-six and had been raised for a lifetime of summer Sundays, broken bikes, baseball games and thumb suckers on a grandmother's old Heriz. She knew good jewelry and what the "back nine" and Uffizi were. She had big breasts and could walk into the Christmas party at Tommy's firm and make easy small talk. These, wrapped in the expectancy of the life he should provide for her, were the dowry she had brought to Tommy Babcock twelve years before.

Her hopes for her marriage had been reasonable: that Tommy's warmheartedness and doggedness—the very qualities that made him a well-liked but mediocre lawyer—would be sufficient to educate their children, pay off the mortgage and buy a little condo at the beach. Now he was sitting with frizzled hair, looking as if baseball were something remote and fundamentally senseless. Elise went to the kitchen.

Stenson, his chin swaddled in gauze, was slumped on the window seat in the breakfast nook. "Hey, Mom, guess what?"

"What?"

"That old guy who was here? He's getting my bike fixed. Vannie told me."

Elise went back to Tommy. "He got Stenson's bike fixed?"

"Yeah. And your car, too. He just called someone, and they came."

Oliver woke up and toddled toward the kitchen. Elise let herself surrender everything to Vannie, who was as taut as a screen door spring and seemed as reliable, too. The children's dinner, the dishes, Oliver's bath, Vannie did them all, while Elise sat with Tommy, watched the game and heard his short, fierce breaths.

At the top of the ninth, he said, "He seems like a decent sort, you know. For all his money, he's just a regular guy."

"So, do you want to go over for drinks?"

"You go, Elise. I don't think I can make it. Give him my apologies. "

"You're sure?"

"One of us should." Tommy pushed himself off the couch.

"Maybe I should just call him and thank him. I can send a bottle of wine tomorrow," she said.

Tommy started toward the stairs in the hallway. "You go. Like I said, he seems a decent sort. He's probably waiting. It's just a drink, Elise. That's all." He rested his hand on the finial. "Just make sure that woman stays. Oliver might wake up while you're gone. And he's getting so heavy." His voice sounded as if it were too weary to come out into the living world. As if it wanted to curl up and stay near his heart.

"Do you need anything?" she asked.

"I'm fine."

She stepped into the hallway.

Tommy took two steps away, up the stairs. "You go, Elise.

He's a decent sort, and there aren't too many of those around. Trust me on that."

She didn't bother changing her shorts. In Charlie Pierce's "Take it," she'd heard a resonance of something inevitable, and, ultimately, fine. Something that told her he'd seen beyond her bloodstained shorts and venal failings. Beyond how she had married Tommy Babcock because Tommy Babcock was handy. Beyond how she was angry he hadn't made partner at the law firm and now she'd inherit less. Beyond how she'd thought about aborting Oliver and still sometimes thought maybe she should have. Beyond how, when Tommy was first diagnosed, she had leapt over hope straight to fatalism. Beyond how the prayers by the new rector of St. David's sounded fatuous. Beyond how she'd already decided that if Molly had one of her nightmares, she'd give her one of Stenson's codeine pills. Or maybe two.

On Charlie's porch was a table with gin and tonic and cut limes, but no glasses.

"You know," Charlie said, "my father only told me three things worth remembering. Wait a minute and I'll tell you about the first." He brought out two frosty glasses. "The first valuable thing Dad told me is that the only way to make a good gin and tonic is to refrigerate your glasses." He put in three cubes.

"What was the second?"

He poured the gin. "Oh, the second was the night before I left for prep school. He came into my room and said 'Remember, Charlie, there are no rules. There are only standards.' "

"And the third, was what?"

He poured the tonic and slipped in a slice of lime. "The third was right after the second. I asked him 'Who sets the standards?' "

"And what did your father tell you?"

"Dad said, 'You do, Charlie. You set the standards.'" He handed her the drink, and she accepted it, having heard in his "standards" a measured modulation telling her Charlie Pierce understood boundaries. And she trusted that about him.

They talked about Stenson's chin. And Vannie's chicken. She thanked him for getting the car fixed. He told her that the fellow fixing Stenson's bike would have it back the next day. She asked him if the man could keep it a little longer.

"I don't want to fight Stenson about riding it with his chin."

"I'll call in the morning." She felt his eyes on her legs.

He asked her if she had any family to help her. She told him she had a married brother in Chicago. And that her parents' divorce was fairly recent and had been nasty. Her mother couldn't get away much from her job on Capitol Hill, and her father and stepmother spent a lot of time at their beach house.

A small woman in pink slippers stepped through the screen door and blinked. She had a sweet nose and a doll's round chin.

"Ginny, this is our neighbor, Elise Babcock. I told you we might be having someone over for drinks."

The woman's small, dry hand had no grip, and when she sat down, she barely dented the cushions. Charlie asked her if she wanted a drink.

"What kind of drink?"

"Gin and tonic."

"No. I don't think so."

"Would you like something else?"

"I don't like gin."

"No. I don't mean anything with gin. Something else."

The woman sighed. "Do we have any root beer? You know I like root beer."

"I'll go see," Charlie said and left.

"I don't know why, but I've always liked root beer," Ginny said.

"Yes, well, soda's good. Especially in the summer," Elise said. "My kids love it."

"Do you have any sisters?"

"No. I wish I did," Elise said.

"Oh." Ginny rubbed her forehead. "My sister never liked root beer."

"Well, different people like different things."

"I like to wear slippers. My feet get sore."

When Charlie came out they chatted a bit more about the heat. Elise said she had to go, and over the head of his wife whose lips were puckered toward her root beer, he said he understood.

◆ ◆ ◆

It wasn't hard. As soon as Stenson's stitches were out, Elise's stepmother called and asked if he and Molly would like to come to the beach. Vannie was coming almost every day, and Oliver liked playing at her feet. Tommy was sleeping more and more.

Charlie told her what to do. It was late afternoon in early August and very, very quiet. Out in a valley of horse farms he waited behind a ramshackle gas station. He held open his car door for her. His Mercedes was old, and he drove with the windows rolled down. Whenever he downshifted, he would flick his other wrist and grab the inside of the steering wheel. She couldn't remember the last time a man had driven her anywhere.

They didn't speak.

He pulled onto a long drive to a big brick house overlooking a meadow. Past the house, he turned onto a dirt road through woods opening to another meadow and a white farmhouse. When they went up the walk he put his hand on her shoulder. The door was unlocked, and the living room had a low ceiling and a big, stone fireplace.

Her earring got caught in her hair. She gave a little a laugh and raised her arms to unfasten it.

He said, "Don't."

He freed her hair. He took her earring off. He cupped her chin to turn her head. He took her other earring off. On a dresser, he laid them side by side. He smelled like lime and wood.

She'd never been undressed by a man who used ceremony to reach her nakedness. He had the touch of a blind man whose sighted fingers could capture the memory of her in their tips. She had soft, pillowy skin, and the impressions his fingers traced were as fleeting as that of a hand dangling from a rowboat on the surface of a lake. But they were disturbances nonetheless.

They didn't speak.

Later, they wrapped themselves in blankets and drank wine on the little porch off the bedroom. He asked about the children. She told him that she regretted she hadn't enrolled Stenson in Pelham Academy. "Tommy and I talked about it, but I just never got around to it."

"Why do you want him to go there?"

"Well, it's all boys. Stenson's smart, but he has all this energy. I think Pelham would channel it a little better than the Pickford School does. It has mostly male teachers. He would do better in a more masculine environment."

"And you think it's too late to get him into Pelham now?"

"They almost never accept anyone this late. Besides, I've already paid Pickford."

Charlie rested one foot on the rusty iron table so that his

blanket fell open. She knew he wanted her to do the same and so she did. He looked at her.

"Today is Monday. Why don't you call Pelham tomorrow afternoon. Not in the morning. Call in the afternoon."

She had her stepmother bring Stenson home from the beach. Pelham Academy interviewed him on Thursday and accepted him on Friday. And the Pickford School refunded the tuition.

"We know how difficult things are right now, Mrs. Babcock," the headmistress said. "The board met and decided to make an exception."

When she went upstairs to tell Tommy, he was asleep in his clothes. His eyelids didn't even flutter when she took off his shoes.

She became obsessed with lotions and ointments. Whenever she had to get a new prescription for Tommy, she'd buy something lily of the valley, or something musk. She bought a thirty-five dollar lipstick and aloe cream for her feet.

It was always the same. The gas station. The silent drive. The solemnity. She sensed that a man lived in the little farmhouse. Her grandfather's apartment had the same desperate orderliness. A recovering alcoholic's space. Everything foursquare. White sheets washed in harsh soap and pulled tight. But she never asked.

If she had and he had told her that a cousin lived there, or that a great aunt owned the estate, she would have probed too far, would have violated the space they allowed themselves, delimited, but bound by no promises or expectations.

They always wrapped themselves in blankets and drank wine on the small, screened porch surrounded by bushes. Someone had hung a hummingbird feeder.

He told her he had a son "doing some ecology work for us in the Adirondacks" and a daughter who owned an art gallery in Palm Beach. He told her he had a law degree, but had never practiced and that he had served on a nuclear submarine and was interested in pre-Columbian North American archaeology. He used to sail and liked Baltimore because it was near Washington, and he tried to "help out the administration in whichever way he could."

When she was home, she never looked at his house. If she saw him getting the mail, she managed to see him for what he was, her gray-haired, next-door neighbor. She began sleeping on a lawn chair she'd moved into the bedroom because she thought Tommy's bones were getting brittle. Nobody had told her that, but, still, she was afraid that if she slept beside him on the bed she'd bump him and break something. She didn't have the time to potty train Oliver and worried that he was "speech delayed." Molly started wetting her bed, and Pelham Academy suggested tutoring in mathematics for Stenson. Her mother came and made lentil soup, but the kids wouldn't eat it. Her stepmother painted Molly's fingernails, and the Pickford School sent a note saying it wasn't allowed. The doctor recommended oxygen for Tommy, so she smoked outside. The whole house could burst into flames.

Tommy kept asking her to bring Oliver to him. He wanted a picture of them together. "I want him to remember me. Molly and Stenson will, but I don't know about Ollie."

When she went to get the pictures, she stopped at a little shop and bought three silk camisoles. They came from France and cost more than her winter coat. When Tommy saw the pictures he cried, and she held and rocked him. "Oh, Tommy, Tommy." She shoved the camisoles behind some ratty sweaters in her dresser.

"I'm going crazy," she told Charlie. It was late October, but still warm.

"No, you're not." The liquid in the hummingbird feeder glinted to red.

"I really think I am. I don't know what I'm doing."

"You have your kids. You're not going to let yourself go."

"I'm so tired. My mother comes when she can. My stepmother. The kids like her, but she smokes and I'm afraid with the oxygen."

"You smoke, Elise."

"Trudi smokes *and* drinks. I'm afraid she'll forget to go outside."

"Just don't have any liquor in the house."

"I want liquor in the house. I'm tired."

"I have something for you." He brought out a strand, a rope, of pearls. She was a tall woman, and they looped below her navel.

"I had a whole speech prepared about how I wanted you to indulge an old man's fantasy," he said. "About how happy it made me to pick these out for you and how, if you didn't accept them, I'd feel just like another foolish, old guy."

"You'll never be foolish, Charlie."

"When it comes to women, all men are foolish. After fifty or so, we only become more foolish. It just gets worse. It's the price we pay for living too long." He ran his hand up and down within the loop. "I only wish I could have given them to you under circumstances where you could enjoy them."

She stopped his hand. "You have to understand, if I seem ungrateful, it's because I'm numb. Nothing's registering. They're exquisite. Really, just exquisite."

"They had to be."

She started to cry. "I haven't been much of a wife, you know. I should have encouraged him to fight harder. I never did. Not once. We never even discussed other options."

He held her head in his hands and kissed her eyelids. When she opened them, a hummingbird was at the feeder. A hovering improbability. He saw it too. The sort of shared transaction that can accumulate to a lifetime.

Two weeks later, Tommy had a nosebleed she couldn't stem, and he went to the hospital. Years later, she would remember calling Vannie and screaming not to do any laundry. She wanted his T-shirts. They were all she had that smelled like him. Early in November, Tommy was moved to the hospice wing.

Someone cooked a turkey and made sweet potatoes. Someone bought a Christmas tree and got Oliver into St. David's preschool. Someone bought him a wooden train and Molly a dollhouse.

In the middle of January, someone bought Stenson his first suit and Elise a black dress. And someone shoveled their walk, so she and the children wouldn't slip the morning they got into the big, waiting car that drove them down St. Bart's Way to St. David's. Maybe Charlie was there. Maybe he wasn't. Elise never could remember.

That February was so cold, even the stars were blue. She was smoking in her back yard, when she heard footsteps crushing the brittle snow. The watch-cap over his ears made Charlie look like what he was: nineteen years older than she was.

"I keep thinking that if I find just the right star, I'll find him. It's crazy," she said.

"You're entitled. It's a crazy time."

"It seems impossible that someone can just stop being. That someone can talk and think one minute and then just not BE. That seems too cruel. If that's true, then everything we do and feel has no purpose at all … we're just accidental muddles of random chemistry. That we go through all of this for nothing."

They were standing so close their blue clouds of breath found each other. "I keep feeling he's out there, somewhere," she said. "I have to believe that." She heard Charlie take another step. "If you touch me, I'll break. I can't let that happen."

"Then I won't touch you."

✦ ✦ ✦

In May, he asked her to lunch at the Center Club, and she bought a new suit. The club had a private elevator, and, over tables covered in stiff, white linens, businessmen murmured to each other as she passed.

"Why here?" she asked.

"It's the safest place. All these old guys think I'm just like them. Someone looking at you and trying to decide which voice in his head he should listen to. The one saying 'Go for it.' Or the one saying, 'You don't stand a chance, you old fool.' They think our meeting is only prelude." He lifted a finger and a waiter came.

Charlie asked about the children, and she told him that the three of them were too careful with each other. "Even my stepmother says they've stopped fighting. They don't play with other kids. In a way, they know too much and that separates them. And sometimes I think … this sounds crazy, but sometimes I think they feel they can make Tommy whole by just being together."

"I have something for you."

When she opened the brown envelope, she saw certificates with blue borders and rows of zeroes.

"Charlie."

He held up his hand. "They're bearer bonds. You should put them in a safe deposit box right away. If you decide to cash them, there's a guy named Burt Greene. He's honest. Honest and cautious. You can trust him."

"Charlie, I can't. I'm not that bad off. Tommy had insurance. And his grandmother says she'll change her will for the kids."

"You're a beautiful woman, Elise. And you're going to become more beautiful. Sorrow can do that to some women. It will to you. Any guy here would want to dazzle you with his money. You don't need that. You're smart, but it's almost impossible to see a man separately from his money. This way, if someone comes along, you can see him for what he is, not as someone to take care of you and the kids. A woman who sees only the money can get overwhelmed. It gets lonely for the guy. Things fall apart." He was looking far out the window and talking to some painful, remembered middle distance.

She waited.

"There's something else," he said. "I've sold the house. My daughter is having some problems down in Florida, and it might be easier this way."

Elise started shoving the envelope back across the table. She didn't want to be bought off with a good-bye gift.

"It's not what you think. If I move, if you want to go on, it might be easier if there's some distance. I'm only human. Think about it. And call Burt Greene."

On the way home, she went to the cemetery, hating the groundskeeper for tipping his hat and assuming she was a devoted widow, when she was only confused, with no more idea of what to do than the robin hopping on Tommy's grave. She ran her fingertips over his marker: Thomas Holcomb Babcock. Beloved Son, Husband, Father. It said everything. And nothing.

In July, she made certain to be down at her father's beach house so she wouldn't see the moving vans, and in October, she met Charlie in Washington. And six months after that, on an estate in Virginia horse country. That next summer, they spent two weeks on a sailboat anchored off Block Island, and when he asked about the children, she told him that Stenson had played shortstop at Pelham and that Molly was friends with the little girl who had moved into his old house. "And Oliver, well, let me just say I don't worry any more about him being speech delayed."

"That's good," he said. He was wearing a baggy old cardigan and wrapped her in it when he hugged her. His neck tasted like salt. When he went for a swim, she touched the sweater, envying it for holding the memory of his bones in its weave. In a drawer under a bunk she found a book of Emily Dickinson's poems inscribed, "To my dear Ginny. Happy Birthday, Charlie."

When she went home, she tried dating other men, but most of them were divorced. She told her stepmother, "We have different sorts of sorrow. I'm wounded one way, and they're in another." People stopped urging her to "move on."

She started working at a decorator's three days a week. When Oliver entered Pelham, the issue of tuition was never brought up, although an anonymous donor had made a "substantial gift" for the new library wing.

She never asked Charlie about it. The foundation they had laid that distant August had been laid in silence, not the absence of noise, but the presence of stillness. To ask, to probe would violate something no less profound for being tacit.

Because San Francisco was cold when they met there, Charlie bought her a mink-lined raincoat. Their room had a view of the Golden Gate, but the fog was so dense they saw only a long, sad drape of gauzy lights. They were having lunch when he got a call from Ginny's clinic in Minneapolis. He said, "I have to go."

On the flight back to Baltimore, Elise sat next to a molecular biologist coming to give a lecture at Hopkins. When he asked her out to dinner she thought she owed it to herself try dating again—somewhere there had to be a man who could give her the sense of steadiness she found with Charlie. But the restaurant was so noisy all she caught from the biologist were bitter slices of "my charming ex-wife." Elise tried telling him about her children, that Stenson had finally buckled down to schoolwork because he wanted his driver's license, that Molly hated her braces, that Oliver was the only fifth grader reading at the ninth-grade level. Across the table, the biologist's smile was rapt, but his eyes didn't understand she was telling him milestones achieved by children dragging a great loss. She didn't even let him kiss her good night.

Stenson and Oliver stopped saying they "felt funny" when she had her father take them to Pelham Academy's annual father-son bull roast, and the hole Tommy's death punched in every holiday began to fill in. At the decorator's, she was showing a client a swatch of rose damask when she noticed the calendar: her wedding anniversary. Three-twenty in the afternoon and she just realized it. Before she went home she got a basket of chrysanthemums for Tommy's grave and noticed his marker no longer looked new and innocent among all the others.

"I was sort of an inattentive wife, and now I'm an indifferent widow," she told Charlie.

"Three kids in twelve years, Elise. You barely had time to say 'Good morning.' You were just constantly adjusting. Reacting," he said. "As for being a widow, there are no rules that I know of."

She touched his arm. "You're a good friend."

It was a drizzly March morning, and they were having

their coffee before a fire in a Manhattan townhouse overlooking Gramercy Park.

"I have to go out for an hour or two. I won't be long," he said. His voice carried a smile—whatever he had to do had nothing to do with Ginny.

When he left, Elise began going through the townhouse. She sensed it was Charlie's truest home, and she wanted to see if she could walk into a room and pick out "his" chair. But she got increasingly restless and started opening drawers, closets. She discovered Ginny everywhere. In little, cracked photographs. Drawers of Belle Isle sweaters. Tubes of cuticle creams. A yellow flowered shower cap.

Despite the drizzle, Elise went and sat in the little park. By spying, she'd betrayed him, and so had diminished herself. He'd never promised her anything and had never asked her for anything she hadn't been willing to give. She'd expected more of herself than to go probing through his things, trying to find how much of him belonged to Ginny, how much to herself. As if he were a pie to be sliced. She owed him more than that. She went back in and was writing him a note saying she'd decided to go home when he returned. He'd bought a puppy. A collie puppy. Its innocence was infectious, so she stayed. They named him Attaboy.

The dog was with them two years later when the October snow in the Adirondacks was powder fine and they cross-country skied. The second day, Charlie fell asleep on the couch before nine. Elise got a blanket to cover him, but his mouth was gaping open, and she didn't want him to know she'd seen him like that. So she wrapped the blanket around herself, pretending to sleep until he got up and kissed her head. "I'm going to bed," he said. Twenty minutes later, when she got in beside him, he was already snoring.

The next afternoon she was heating stew when Charlie said that Stenson should think about going to Annapolis.

She poured the stew into speckled metal bowls. "He's a gung-ho sort of kid. You know that. He'd like it, but the Academy's hard to get into."

"He should try. Have him try." He poured some stew for Attaboy.

◆ ◆ ◆

Stenson was serving on a submarine, the rainy April morning Charlie called and Elise heard the resonance of an inward turning. She packed and went to New York. From across the room overlooking Gramercy Park, she saw the effort he made to smile when he saw the pearls. Under silver dishes blue flames burned. He pulled out her chair. They hardly spoke.

"I wanted to get you something," he said over coffee. "Something significant, but all the jewelers said they needed more time. I was only diagnosed a few days ago."

"Oh, Charlie." On the white tablecloth, her hand looked old and hoary.

"I'm seventy-one, Elise. Prostate cancer doesn't leave a man much to brag about. If you're lucky, you live a little longer. If you're very lucky you live and you don't piss yourself. If you're very, very lucky, you live, you don't piss yourself, and you get to hold onto your manhood. All the money in the world can't buy that kind of luck. Not for me."

When she told him there were new treatments, new procedures, her voice sounded shrill and she hated it.

"What good is treatment," he said, "if you can't even recognize yourself when it's through? I don't want to be an old fool pining for past glories."

She took his hand and kissed it.

"Elise."

174

"What?"

"I want you to go."

"What? No!" He had never asked her for anything she hadn't been willing to give, but now he was asking for everything, for breath itself.

"They say some women only know themselves by the affirmation they receive from the eyes of men," he said.

"I don't know what you're talking about," she lashed and hated herself for slapping him with a pained, bitter lie.

"Yes you do. It's not that much different with a man. You have no idea how many times I remember you walking into a room, looking for me and giving off that something that says you're a woman who's found her man. A man needs an affirmation, too. At least, I do. From you. I couldn't stand to have you walk into a room and see pity in your eyes."

"I'd never pity you, Charlie." She was leaving him nothing but lies, after they'd been so honest with each other, never speaking what they gave each other, never needing to.

"You won't be able to help but pity me. I'm becoming someone different, and you won't be able to look at me without remembering what I had been. Soon enough I'll be surrounded by well-intended, but pitying eyes. I don't need yours, too."

Someone covered the blue flames. Someone carried away the silver dishes. She wanted to say something calm, something memorable—he had enough on his mind without worrying that she was going to fall apart. He had to trust she'd hold herself together.

When she draped her scarf, the pearls swung. "They say something else, too, you know," she said.

"What?"

She put on her coat. "They say that we only love the feelings, not the person. We just love the feelings, because we can't ever really know another person. Not entirely." She picked up

175

her handbag. "If that's true, if I just loved the feeling you gave me, not you, well, I hope, I pray, it was enough. With all my heart, I pray that. The feeling was wonderful."

"It was everything to me," he said.

✦ ✦ ✦

By the time the train crossed from New Jersey into Delaware the rain had ended, and by the time it crossed the Susquehanna River night had nearly fallen. To the west, only the faintest scatterings of violet and gold bobbed on the river, and to the east, where it emptied into the Chesapeake, the river and bay were a meld of gray. Little lights dotted the shore. Sometimes a low roofline.

Closer to Baltimore, the houses were only a blur of the city's famous ox-blood red brick rowhouses. One after another, with narrow little yards ending at concrete alleys. Sometimes she could make out a dog. A basketball hoop. A bike. And the windows. In some, yellow lights.

Behind all of them, she knew, were dreams and disappointments. Generations, accreting one after another, like the soot burrowing into the bricks, slowly corroding the concrete holding them one to the other. Her losses, she knew, were no greater than those in any of the tiny houses. And her loves, no more worthy. She was almost as old as Charlie had been the afternoon he had stepped through her hedge.

When the train stopped, the cavernous station's ceiling was an echo chamber catching every sound and sending it ricocheting off the oak waiting-room benches and terrazzo floor. On the sidewalk in front, over the sibilance of wheels slicing the wide boulevards' dampness and the cabbies' barking, she heard a frail young man with a wispy red beard and knitted turquois beret playing a Peruvian pan pipe. Beside him, in a concrete planter, a random jumble of daffodils bobbed and danced. Elise opened her purse, tossed a few dollars into the basket at the piper's feet and got into a cab.

"Take me home," she told the driver. "Take me home."

THE OTHER BETTY

G row old and you'll become a stranger to yourself. Trust me. The day will come when even your own reflection is unrecognizable to you.

This morning, the windows of the bakery-cum-coffee shop below my condo reflect a face not my own, but one resurrected from the five-generation depth of my gene pool. Those elongated ears, that predominant chin, they belong to my father's great-grandmother. And her obsidian eyes, whoever set them in my skull? They were in her portrait over the dining room highboy on St. Bart's Way, where they glared at me and my little sister, the two of us, our laps blanketed by Irish linen napkins and feeling privileged to be having dinner in the dining room with our parents and not the kitchen.

I tell Ramir, whose shop it is, just my usual croissant and cup of hazelnut, and thank you.

"Decaf, Ms. Margot?" Ramir's eyes are triumphant that he, not I, has recalled what's good for me.

"Yes, yes, decaf." Let him have his little victory. I'm tired and rattled: being awake since before dawn does that. The morning traffic hadn't started yet when I opened my eyes and saw a memory. Of a kiss. As surely as I once saw my husband Walter knotting his tie in the dim morning light, I saw that kiss. I girded myself with composure when Walter died; for three months I had my hairdresser come to my house. My manicurist, too. I'm tall and can carry off the kick-pleated skirt and boots I'm wearing. The mink vest, my gift to myself for my sixty-fifth birthday, is possibly too soigné. I don't know.

I'm afraid I'm losing perspective. As the roles I once played fade, so does my sense of appropriate costuming. Twelve years of Briarley School jumpers, then a bouquet of ball gowns. And, of course, the ultimate one, the white one, followed by three sets of maternity clothes and decades-worth of good suits and sensible travel wear.

Now, Walter's gone, the children grown, and the memories of those roles recede, while more elemental ones, like that kiss, surface, leaving me to question if those parts I played were roles at all and not accretions to protect that smart, wary girl who grew up with her little sister on St. Bart's Way.

In a battered old briefcase that Walter gave me when I ran the tutorial program at St. David's, I have my newspaper and an album of old family pictures. After my coffee I'll drive out to the consignment shop where my sister works and show her the album. The one picture in particular.

It's mid-morning, and inside the bakery the little metal tables and chairs are canted at angles of absence. The weathermen have driven people into a frenzy by predicting snow, and the air almost undulates with the aftermath of their anxiety. Ramir comes over, sets my croissant and coffee down. Then does something he's never done in the two years I've had my condo: he pulls out the chair opposite mine. He doesn't sit, but looks at me expectantly. "May I?"

What can I say? That it's not really convenient? That I need this time alone to decide what I'm going to tell my sister about that kiss? That I never was a person who welcomed unexpected intimacies? I smile. "Of course, please do, Ramir."

His own smile is an admixture of self-assertion and discomfort. Even though the realignment of the borders between us is his idea, he's not at ease.

My seventieth birthday present to myself was a telescope. I thought the time had come to understand the whirling gavotte of the stars. A dance I sometimes think of as a waltz of souls.

But I made the mistake of telling Ramir and found that with his intimate Hindu knowledge of astrology he doesn't so much talk as gossip about the constellations.

"So did you see Orion last night?" he asks.

"Not last night. I got to reading."

"Oh, but you should have seen it. Magnificent, I tell you. Just magnificent. What could have kept you from that?"

"The Battle of Midway. I'm concentrating on the Pacific theater now."

"Oh, Ms. Margot. You and your history. What's history but the study of man's inhumanity to man? But the stars, the stars, now they are our path, aren't they? Our path to wherever." He stops, embarrassed for his outburst.

"Well, maybe I'll look tonight."

"Yes, but the snow... you'll miss it. That belt of Orion's, last night, that was something, I tell you."

What Ramir doesn't know is that most of my knowledge of the constellations comes from Google. I had no time for stars once I discovered ships.

From all over the world, they plow into old Baltimore's harbor. And at the oddest hours, like clandestine lovers. Floating worlds that, secreted away in my condo, I am privy to, like a voyeur prying into universes of men, an unseemly compulsion. No one but my sister knows I watch them; she's the only one who understands my private clairvoyance. Ramir is a proper man; I suspect he almost certainly would not approve. "One of my aunts back in Goa," he says, getting, I sense, to what is his real business, "has sent me a new chai. An espe-cially delicate Oolong with a touch of cinnamon and cumin. Probably other things in it, too. Its calming properties are sup-posedly fantastic. Really fantastic."

"Ah, yes, calming properties," I smile at him. He's an as-tute, sensitive man, and he's probably offering "calming prop-erties" because he's noticed the tightness in my jaw, the rigidity of my shoulders this morning.

"The box has a message advising you to hold the cup in your palms," he continues, "for three minutes before putting it to your lips. Three minutes, no less."

"And does the box advise you what do during that time? Count the seconds?"

There's a slight contraction in his eyes; my tone's mockery has wounded him, but Ramir lets it pass. "Well, yes, if you want. Or contemplate the tea. Just one hundred eighty seconds. Half a circle, that's all. Would you like to try it, Miss Margot?"

He's so earnest, what can I say? I get out my newspaper and wait. Ramir brings the tea brewing in a little pot so per-fectly yellow it could be a porcelain buttercup. "Let it soak a bit," he says and leaves me.

I feel that if I am going to count the seconds, I should do so with my eyes closed, but an old woman holding a teacup with her eyes shut could look frail or worse to the other cus-tomers. I get up to move around to the chair vacated by Ramir and bump the one with my briefcase. The album spills out and the picture of The Other Betty, as I've dubbed her, skitters out across the floor and under a table. I am a mess of awkwardness as I extract it. More than six decades buried, and now, from the bakery floor, she smiles a smile that makes you want to know her. Or maybe *be* her. Big boned, she's wearing a polka-dot dress cinched at the waist and open at the neck. On our front porch on St. Bart's Way, she leans back against the railing, each arm extending away from her body so that the railing, her arms, and her body form matching isosceles triangles of bright afternoon light. She looks happy. And almost aggressively confident. On the back, I read my mother's elegant handwriting: "Betty, September, 1944."

Taking in boarders wasn't something done on St. Bart's Way, but when the war came those big houses seemed self-indulgent, especially with so many workers cramming into Baltimore for jobs. I remember my father had already gone to the Navy, and my mother was alone. In my memory she's always standing, silhouetted against the parlor's windows, her arms wrapped around herself. She never scolded, in fact, she scarcely talked. Whatever I wanted, her only answer was, "Not now, Margot. Not now."

And then came Betty with her easy, loud laugh. Her beer. Her cigarettes. Her music.

"You certainly are a quietest little girl I've ever met, Twerp," she said the afternoon she pinned my braids to the top of my head like a crown. "Look. See, on top they make your eyes stand out. Emphasize what you've got, Twerp. That's what I say. You don't want to go around looking all hangdog."

She had come from Western Maryland, the coal mining Appalachian part of the state where tiny, desperate towns hugged mountainsides like workhouse children clinging to their mother's knees. Only one person, somehow she filled our whole house. Every morning, when she hopped on the streetcar, she left just enough energy behind to get my mother going out to her victory garden, or volunteering at the Red Cross, or even jumping rope with me. But by evening we'd both be looking forward to the door banging wide and Betty's being home.

I settle into the chair vacated by Ramir, set aside my coffee, pour the tea, and close my eyes and let its warmth draw my hands to the cup. But, I have to pull them away; it's too hot.

Still, I keep my eyes closed and try to visualize the warm pillow of air between palms and cup: the space feels saffron. I sniff for the cumin, and when I open my eyes, I'm surprised to see that I have raised the cup to my lips. I sip. Comfort washes around my tongue and down my throat. I close my eyes again and try to think of what to tell my sister, but my mind is a paisley swirl of memory and the momentary pleasure of tea.

"So, did you like it, Ms. Margot? The tea?" Ramir says when I go to the register.

"It's wonderful. Give me two boxes. One for my sister."

"Ah, yes, your sister. She'll enjoy it, I'm sure." His remark heavy with understanding for how much my sister needs calming properties. I'd raved about his shop to her, and the first time she'd come to it, all blowsy, ironic persona and clacking jewelry, she'd enchanted Ramir by recounting how she'd lived on the beach in Goa. "It was the sixties. If you weren't in an ashram, you were in nowhere land." The second time she wore a Kashmiri paisley shawl that enthralled him only more. But the third time, she and Don, the man she lives with in a rickety old farmhouse, had spent the afternoon at a bar in Fells Point. She wanted to order a birthday cake for me, but couldn't remember if I liked angel food or not. When she called me from the bakery to find out, her voice was slush spilling from the receiver, and I sailed down from my condo to collect her and Don. But for weeks afterwards. Ramir's face held the stricken expression of someone caught in an anguish of embarrassment.

He never knew the worst of it. How our father had had to go to Goa to bring my sister home, and the months of hospitalizations that followed: her infected body, her fractured mind. As for the Kashmiri shawl, she stole it. From our mother. Who lay in the next room. Mummified by morphine.

Ramir starts to tally up my tea and I ask him for three raspberry and three lemon tarts and then three éclairs — one or two of Don's grown sons stay at the farmhouse, sometimes, men almost large enough to swallow an éclair whole.

As I leave the shop, a woman with two little brightly bundled girls goes in. I catch her eye and we exchange that quick smile of women sharing a moment of maternal commiseration. Suddenly I know what I want. I want to go to St. Bart's Way.

I drive with the pastries in back and the album sitting on the seat next to mine to a neighborhood where everything flows: wide porch railings into a series of six-over-six windows, and then into weathered shingles and then fieldstone chimneys.

My parents belonged to the neighborhood's second generation. By the time they bought our home, the ivy had almost camouflaged the foundation and the slate on the roof had a dusting of moss. My mother had a hunger for light, but our yard's trees were already tall, so throughout the day she'd follow the sun's course from window to window.

I remember she was at the ones in the parlor, the afternoon I came running up the sidewalk. "We just dropped an Adam bomb on the Japs," I shouted. "Billy Walters just told me." The gauzy summer curtains over the open windows were rising and falling. The Other Betty wasn't home from work yet and my mother was alone. She held one arm across her stomach, her palm cradling her other elbow. She inhaled her cigarette so deeply, I think she wanted to disappear in smoke. When she turned from the window she looked at me as if I were some stranger's child. "I guess that means your father will be home, soon," she said. "Everything will be over now." The curtains suddenly fluttered higher, three white ripples. "I think we might have a storm." Then she smiled. "It will clear the air."

Once our parents were dead, the house was sold. But a

few years later, when a For Sale sign was hung on it again, I felt cheated, almost as if some understanding had been violated, as if the house was never to change hands without my permission. And now it's for sale again. Beneath the realtor's oval green sign hangs a cylinder holding fliers of vital statistics. When I get out to get one for my sister, the air has the ozonic scent of pre-snow, and it feels colder than when I left Ramir's. I should just leave, I think. I'll drop the pastries off for St. David's coffee hour so they won't go to waste, go home and tell my sister that I didn't want to get caught in the snow. She'll understand. I just want to peek in the sunroom and leave. I get into my car and pull into the drive, get out and walk past the side window of our father's old study to the sunroom. Except for a faded canvas camp chair, it's empty.

I'm backing out of the drive, when I have to slam on my brakes to avoid hitting a car pulling in. The practiced smile of the woman who steps out can't hide her eyes' irritation. She's carrying a briefcase and a bouquet of periwinkle freesia.

"You're early," she says.

I lower my window. "What?"

Her smile never wavers. "Are you Claudia Marburg from Minneapolis?"

"No. I'm Margot Hart from Baltimore and I'm afraid you've caught me trespassing." Looking up at her makes me feel diminished. "I was taking a forbidden trip down Memory Lane. This is the house I grew up in, and I let nostalgia get the best of me. I'm sorry."

Her hair is brittle blonde, and against the glowering sky her flowers look vaingloriously giddy. She shifts them to her other arm. "I'm waiting to show it to a woman flying in from Minneapolis. Her husband's just taken an appointment at Hopkins."

"Again, I'm terribly sorry." I wonder if she's thinking of calling the police. "If you could just back up, I'll be gone." I feel her assessing my grey hair, my aged chin.

Her eyes melt a little. "No harm. At open houses, people come back and visit their old places all the time."

She starts toward her car, and I have to raise my voice. "I especially wanted to see the sunroom. F. Scott Fitzgerald loved sitting there. He said it relaxed him." She stops; I've reeled her in.

"F. Scott Fitzgerald used to come here?"

"When Zelda was in treatment." I open the album and show her a picture of our Uncle Ward, mustached and ascotted and with one foot on the running board of a roadster. "Our father was a lawyer," I say, "and I'm not certain how he knew Fitzgerald, although I clearly remember him in the sunroom." Then, before the realtor has a chance to look too closely, I shut the album.

"I'm Kathy Paulson," she smiles down at me. "It you want to come in and look around, I don't see any harm. My client isn't due for half an hour. The Fitzgerald connection, what with St. Paul and all, she'll probably be interested in that. People love to know a house's history."

I leave the album in my car and follow her around to the front. While she fumbles with the lockbox and I hold her flowers, she goes on about how a house's connection to someone famous adds value. She isn't certain why. The house that Spiro Agnew owned sold for nearly a third more than an identical one down the street. And you don't want to know about Barry Levinson's parents' place.

I don't know how long I can keep up my Fitzgerald lie, so when we're in the foyer, I substitute the truth: I tell her about Mencken coming to dinner. Although I leave out how he was already in eclipse by the time he sat under our father's great-grandmother's portrait. Nor do I tell her about the terrible spanking our father had given my sister just before Mencken came. Or how our mother grabbed our father's arm, saying, "No, Fred, not the belt." Or how my sister sat sobbing beside me at the kitchen table while our parents ate with Mencken.

Kathy Paulson explains that the house is on the market because of a divorce—"Real nasty"—and she's had a hard time persuading either party to leave any furniture behind. What's left looks as worn as the camp chair in the sunroom. She heads toward the kitchen, but I stop in the parlor. I remember standing on a hassock by the window, The Other Betty on a couch, watching my mother pin up the hem of a jumper she'd sewn for me. I remember my mother touching my leg so I'd turn and her muttering through a mouthful of pins, "I don't know what I would have done without you, Betty. I never knew what it could be like." Betty got up, cupped my mother's chin to turn her face to her own, and said, "You'd have figured it out, Lil. You'd have figured it out."

I go down the hall to the kitchen, but nothing is familiar. All the cabinets are white, and an island with a breakfast bar stretches across the middle where our table used to be.

The night I had come down for a drink of water, I immediately saw that someone had committed a violation. The table had been moved against the stove. I was so startled by this displacement that I just stayed in the dark hallway. On the counter, beside an open bottle, a Victrola held its needle deep in a record's groove, and cigarette smoke shimmied up to the weak light over the void left by the table. A white arm flashed into the doorway frame. Then a bare leg. Then I saw my mother. Laughing. In her slip. And then The Other Betty, in hers. I went back upstairs.

Kathy Paulson is fussing with her freesia. She puts them on the island, gives a wry smile: Too obvious. Then she sets

them on the end of the marble counter and smiles again, satis-
fied. I tell her that my father and his Yale pals used to gather
out in the sunroom and sing "The Whiffenpoof Song." "We
had a piano out there."

Her smile widens, "I guess they didn't sing Whiffenpoof
with Fitzgerald around. He was Princeton, wasn't he?"

I feel overheated in my vest. "Yes. I think so."

"Yale buddies … Fitzgerald … it's all good. You take your
time, and I'll move my car so you can back out."

The sunroom is off the dining room, where I stay until I
hear the front door close. Then I move to the sunroom.

A fierce thunderstorm had sent me searching for my
mother. I had wandered through most of the house without
finding either her or Betty. I don't know why I hadn't checked
the sunroom earlier. Maybe I wanted to prolong the terror of
searching in the dark. I've always found something delicious
about the danger of a dark house. Or maybe the memory of
those slip dancers told me I didn't really want to find her.

When I did, she was on a wicker couch. With Betty, who
was wearing her polka dot dress. But Mother was in her slip
again. And Betty was kissing her. Holding her, bending her
head back. Kissing her. That's the memory I awoke to this
morning.

When I step onto the front porch, I have to clench my teeth
to keep them from chattering, whether from the cold or the tor-
ment of memory, I can't tell. As I'm going down the front steps
Kathy Paulson is coming up. "I almost wish you'd stay so you
could tell my client all your wonderful stories."

"I can't … I can't … the snow. I'd love to, but the snow.
Good luck with your client. Thank you … thank you." I slip
into my car and pull away.

The Other Betty was gone for good, and my father had
been home from the Navy since Halloween. Summer again,

and the whole house swarmed with aunts and uncles because my mother was coming home, too, coming home from the hospital. With my little sister. My new little sister. The words were like a refrain playing in my brain. I couldn't get away from them, but I didn't know what they meant. I couldn't locate the place in my heart where "my little sister" was supposed to reside.

And then my mother was in the sunroom. She was holding my sister who was wrapped so mysteriously I felt paralyzed. My father picked me up and sat me on the wicker couch. "Way back, Margot," he said. "Sit way back." And he laid my sister across my lap and I stared into profound grey eyes looking into mine.

"She can't see anything yet," someone said. But I knew that wasn't true. My sister's eyes were saying "You and me. You and me. Against all others." And then she did something so unexpected, I laughed. She yawned. A deep, gasping yawn that showed her wiggly little tongue thrashing around in her mouth. Such audacity in front of everyone. I'd heard more than once since my father had come home: "Cover your mouth, Margot. If you must let out a yawn, at least cover your mouth." But my sister's mouth was so wide I imagined I could look down her throat and see her tiny, pounding heart. And then her little body settled more deeply into my lap and she continued looking at me, and I knew that the place in my heart where she resided was all of it.

After our father's mother, she was christened Elizabeth, but her name quickly morphed, first, briefly, into Beth, and then into the name on her cake by her second birthday: Betty. Until this morning I never saw any connection, but now I think perhaps my mother was attempting to recreate The Other Betty. Who knows how much of my sister's rebellious streak sprang from her own nature and how much was engendered by my mother's encouragement. My own somber nature Mother probably considered too fixed, but my sister was a *tabula rasa* on which she could imprint the liberation she'd experienced during that passionate interlude. Maybe she thought she could relive that freedom through my sister.

My sister delighted in flouting all the conformity, obligations and expectations that went with the St. Bart's Way of life. And sometimes she succeeded in delighting others too, especially our mother. When she was eight she sang "Mambo Italiano," at our parents' Christmas party. When she was ten she sent her tardy Christmas thank-you notes as Easter cards. When she was twelve she got Rastafarian braids when we vacationed in Jamaica.

But as she grew older, her transgressions grew bolder and drove our parents, especially our father, to distraction. And then to rages. Phone calls began from the Briarley School followed by hastily written donation checks. Then, in my sister's senior year, in the days before Roe. v. Wade, there was the sudden trip to Puerto Rico. Then there were the failing grades from Hollins College. Then from the University of Maryland. And then my father throwing up his hands saying, "That's it. I'm done." But, of course, he went to Goa and collected her. And I was so grateful. Who else but my sister could I hand my bouquet to the day I turned to Walter before the altar in St. David's?

The little shop where she works is on an old main road that once connected Baltimore with Pennsylvania. Decades ago, a quick ribbon of highway was laid through rolling farmland to sweep the traffic from one state to another, and the old main road became a sleepy afterthought littered with fast food restaurants, hair salons and tire stores. But a few miles of the original one-story structures have managed to maintain them-

THE OTHER BETTY

selves as antique shops, or, in the case of the one where Betty
works, a consignment shop.

I think Don's sister got her the job, or maybe someone from
AA. All I know is that she's been happy among other people's
castoffs and has become quite expert in spotting pieces of true
value, especially jewelry. I wish I'd worn the enamel brooch
she gave me last Christmas, and think of stopping to get something to bring for lunch, but decide to settle for one of the pack-
ets of noodles I know she keeps in her desk

Ramir's pastries and my briefcase weigh me down when
I struggle with the door. But Betty comes bouncing from the
back in aquamarine Crocs and a tartan jumper. *Papier mâche*
sailfish dangle from her ears.

I had thought the kiss could explain the kinked chain of
her life, shattered marriages, shattered children—one lost in
Las Cruces, one trying to "make it" by teaching scrapbooking.
I thought I'd tell her about the kiss and she'd see a causal link
between our mother's abandon and her own lifelong quest for
release, but now I don't know what to say.

"You won't believe what's come," she says. Among the
faded slipcovers and dull pewter, my sister is the one bit of
bright. "A telescope. I want your opinion. I'm thinking of getting it for Don."

"For Don? Why?" The scope she heads toward is brass,
not a good sign. Brass usually is the indication of an ornament.

"It's all your fault, you know," my sister says. "You remember that time we were getting your birthday cake and you
came and brought us up to your condo? Well, Don really en-
joyed yours."

I set down the pastries, the tea, and my briefcase and fasten
the telescope on the telephone line outside the window where
a row of pigeons sits wing-to-wing, huddled against the com-

191

ing storm. When I look through the eyepiece, the claw of one could be a crosshatched map of the world.

"It's pretty good," I say.

"I get twenty percent off," she says. "And Don's birthday is coming up." She nods to the bag with Ramir's tea and pastries. "What's that?"

"I thought you could heat up some of those high-sodium noodles. And then have lemon tarts. Or raspberry, too. And I bought some tea."

"Nuts to the noodles. This old tart is skipping right to *her* tarts."

"Well, at least plug in the pot for tea."

We sit, the two of us, among a jumble of gate leg tables and wing backed chairs. Betty grabs a bundle of linen napkins and hands me one. On the corner, in royal blue, someone has embroidered the initials D. W. I almost choke on the misbegotten efforts spent on all this accumulation.

"I went to the house," I tell her.

"What? Why?"

"Oh, I don't know … nostalgia, I guess." Out the window, the first flakes have begun falling. "It's for sale again. I almost slammed into the realtor in the driveway." I tell her about how I lied. "I said F. Scott Fitzgerald used to love to come sit in our sunroom."

"You didn't."

"She's a realtor, for heaven's sake, Betty. It's not like she never lied." Perhaps I should stop here. Who's to say there's a causal connection between The Other Betty and my sister? But showing off my own cleverness has always been a weakness of mine. "I even passed off a picture of Uncle Ward as Fitzgerald."

My sister fingers her napkin. "But why did you happen have a picture of Uncle Ward with you?"

She's caught me. I have to go on and tell her about the kiss. But what good will it do? Who's to say that the errors she's made in her life are any greater than the ones I made in mine when I played the caring wife and mother but hid my withholding heart. In the office, the electric pot is screaming, and when my sister comes back from unplugging it, I've taken out the picture of The Other Betty. The photo is square with a wide scalloped border and when she takes it, my sister curls her index finger against her thumb, and then snaps it against the picture. "Betty," she says. "Betty from Lonaconey."

"You know?"

"I'm her namesake.'You were named for a dear, dear friend,' Mom told me. I was twelve, maybe thirteen. But I didn't know exactly *how* dear until Mom was dying. This isn't the only picture, you know. There were others."

"Where?"

"In the letters she sent to Mom."

"What letters?"

Across the shop, a jack-in-the-box has a manic grin that I want to slap off.

"In that shawl I took, the one you threw such a fit about. A whole bundle was wrapped in it. All postmarked Lonaconey. All from Betty. Very, very steamy, I must say. You said you brought tea?"

"But you've known about Mom and her since then and you didn't say anything?"

"What would I say, Margot? That our mother couldn't be with the person who probably was her truest love? That her whole life was a lie? I don't even know if that's true. Who knows anything?"

But why didn't you tell me?"

"You know, you dig too much, Margot. You always have. Sometimes I think that you think that everything that's ever going to happen already has. I just wanted the shawl. I didn't know there were any letters. And, then, when I did, I didn't know what to do with them."

"So, what did you?"

"I burned them. Rather, Don did."

"He burned them?"

"He said they were bad karma. So he burned them. If you want I've got some tea in my drawer."

"But why did he just go ahead and do that?"

"He didn't 'just go ahead,' Margot. He did it because he saw they were upsetting me. So we opened a bottle of wine, he made a fire, and he burned them."

Her face is flushed. I've done that to her.

"No. No. Use this." I hand her Ramir's tea.

When she goes toward the office, I look through the scope again. If it weren't snowing, Don could see Orion's belt tonight. But perhaps he and my sister have better things to do than study the stars. She comes back with a teapot and two cups on a silver tray.

"One of the benefits of working here, is you get to use nice stuff." She sets the tray on a marble console and settles into a rocking chair with upholstered arms.

"The one I feel sorry for is Dad," she says.

"Dad?"

"Think of it. He had to know something was wrong. Who knows… maybe he knew about Mom and Betty. At the very least he had to know Mom wasn't the same woman he left when he went into the Navy."

I smile at her. "Who's to say? Maybe she was better."

"No. I don't think so. Those letters … what she and Betty had. Part of her had to be always longing for that."

She pours the tea, and I tell her how we're supposed to close our eyes, hold the tea and wait three minutes before drinking. The silence of the snow is deep and benign. White flakes beyond enumeration falling on an old, weary city. I think of our mother, her daily orbit to the windows of our house, her unexpected passion, and of our father, his rages, perhaps at her mysterious remove. Or perhaps not. Who's to say? So here we sit, my sister and me, two old women entwined at the root. Each counting out our half circle of time amid scents of cinnamon and cumin. Comfort enough. Yes, comfort enough.

Final Note

The characters, institutions and incidents in these stories are all fictions, and any resemblance to actual people, places or occurrences in Baltimore is purely coincidental. The same is true of St. Bart's Way: the street exists only in my imagination.

ACKNOWLEDGMENTS

The stories of *St. Bart's Way* never would have been published without the helpful suggestions from a group of writers who met regularly over the course of several years. Some belonged to the group for only a few months; others for much longer, but I'm grateful to each for their well-considered criticism, encouraging comments and the example they set by their own dedication to writing. So thank you to Andria Cole, Barbara Diehl, Kathy Flann, Mimi Godfrey, Nate Haken, Ashley Kaufman, James Magruder Susan McCullum-Smith, Lara McLaughlin, Jen Mikalski, Liz Moser, Susan Muaddi Darraj, Lalita Noronha, Meredith Pooler, Rosalia Scalia, and Todd Whaley.

I also wish to thank the editors and staffs of the following journals and reviews for publishing these stories individually: *Artisan* for publishing "Bellini's Brush"; *Dalhousie Review* for "Abiding Blue Velvet"; *The Distillery* for "After the Service"; *The Floating Holiday* for "Prime Meridian"; *The Georgetown Review* for "Other Men's Sons"; *Left Curve* for "The Haint"; *Passages North* for "The Assembly"; *Potpourri* for "The Crunch"; *Scribble* for "Firewalker" and "Standards"; *Timber Creek Review* for "Near Sunset"; and *Transcendent Visions* for "Bang!".

I also am profoundly grateful to the team at Washington Writers' Publishing House for choosing *St. Bart's Way* as the winner for its 2015 fiction award, and for their patience and astute editorial input throughout the publication process.

Finally, my thanks go to my friend Anne Barnes, whose input helped these stories along and to Ellen Clair Lamb for her amazing proofreading skills.

www.ingramcontent.com/pod-product-compliance
Lightning Source LLC
Chambersburg PA
CBHW020329260626
47156CB00004B/1436